THE
SCOTS MAGAZINE,
AND
GENERAL INTELLIGENCER.

NEMO ME IMPUNE LACESSET

JANUARY, 1739.

To be continued every Month. Price Sixpence each.

CONTAINING,

N. B. *As it is proposed to make this Magazine a complete Chronicle of the Time from its commencement, we shall not insert any Political Debates, till we can offer those of the current year; which will be continued with all possible care from the time of our beginning them, in the month of* July.

EDINBURGH: Printed by W. SANDS, A. BRYMER, A. MURRAY and J. COCHRAN. Sold by the Booksellers in Town and Country, and at the Printing-house in *Burnet's* Close. MDCCXXXIX.

The contents page of the very first *Scots Magazine*.

THE SCOTS MAGAZINE

A Celebration of 250 Years

PELHAM BOOKS/Stephen Greene Press

THE SCOTS MAGAZINE
1739–1989 – The world's oldest Popular Periodical
A celebration of 250 years

PELHAM BOOKS/Stephen Greene Press

Published by the Penguin Group
27 Wrights Lane, London W8 5TZ, England
Viking Penguin, a division of Penguin Books USA Inc., 375 Hudson Street, New York,
New York 10014, USA
The Stephen Greene Press, 15 Muzzey Street, Lexington, Massachusetts 02173, USA
Penguin Books Australia Ltd, Ringwood, Victoria, Australia
Penguin Books Canada Ltd, 2801 John Street, Markham, Ontario, Canada L3R 1B4
Penguin Books (NZ) Ltd, 182–190 Wairau Road, Auckland 10, New Zealand
Penguin Books Ltd, Registered Offices: Harmondsworth, Middlesex, England

First published 1989 (hardback), 1990 (paperback)

Made and printed in Scotland by Bell & Bain Ltd, Glasgow

Typeset by Cambridge Photosetting Services

Origination by Anglia Graphics, Bedford

A CIP catalogue record for this book is available from the British Library.

ISBN 0 7207 1989 5

CONTENTS

FICTION
A powerful short story set in winter.

Melrose, the finest and best-known of our ruined abbeys. Founded in 1136 it was presented to the nation by the Duke of Buccleuch in 1918. PHOTO: DOUGLAS LAIDLAW

CONTRIBUTORS

John MacLeay was born in Glasgow, regards Cowal as his home, but has lived in Cornwall since 1970. Occupations have included folksinger, portrait artist and hotelier.

Bob Morrow spent his working life in a brickworks. The necessary balance was restored by his activities as a semi-professional musician. In retirement he started an entirely new career as a writer.

Lea MacNally was born in Fort Augustus. He was a professional deerstalker until appointed warden/naturalist on the National Trust for Scotland's property in Torridon. He is the author of several books on Highland wildlife.

Dr James Fleming McHarg is a Fellow of the Royal College of Physicians of Edinburgh and a Founder Fellow of the Royal College of Psychiatrists. He has published works in the fields of psychiatry, neurology, parapsychology and the history of medicine in Scotland.

Gordon McCulloch entered the University of Stirling as a mature student and emerged with a First in English and Folklife Studies. He has returned to his original profession as a draughtsman, but continues his folklore studies.

Robin Shaw was educated at Kilsyth and the Universities of Glasgow and Washington, USA. He has written a novel, *Running*, a book on mountaineering and one on batik.

W. D. Bernard is a professional musician. He was in charge of the Music Department at Forfar Academy 1933–67. Hobbies include tape-recording, hill-walking and photography and he has filmed several Scottish rivers from source to the sea.

Archie McKerracher has been contributing articles to *The Scots Magazine* since 1971. His researches have led him into investigating many unusual aspects of Scottish history. The author of two books on Perthshire, he lives in Dunblane.

Ken Andrew is a dedicated walker and climber who has ascended all the Munros, Corbetts and Donalds. He is the author of several books on the south of Scotland and the official guide to the Southern Upland Way.

Dorothy K. Haynes was a prolific contributor of articles and short stories to *The Scots Magazine*. Many of her stories have been anthologised and two collections were published as well as three novels. She lived in Lanark up to her death in 1987.

Margaret MacDougall's first job was as a journalist on *The Glasgow Herald*. She is presently working in an Edinburgh bookshop.

J. L. Goskirk gave up architecture to study for the ministry of the Church of Scotland. He occupies the linked charge of Lairg and Rogart in Sutherland.

Alex R. Mitchell was born at Clydebank and is steeped in Glasgow humour. He was for 46 years on the editorial staff of *The Sunday Post* and *Weekly News*. He has written countless scripts for Scots stars including Tommy Morgan, Rikki Fulton and Stanley "Parliamo Glasgow" Baxter.

Rennie McOwan lives in Stirling. He is a fulltime writer and broadcaster concentrating mainly on history, tourism, environmental and other outdoor topics. He also writes children's books and is a popular lecturer.

Martin Moran is a native of North Shields, Tyneside. He has climbed in the Alps, the Himalaya and in other countries, but is happiest in the Highlands. He and his wife Joy run a climbing school at Lochcarron, Wester Ross.

Tom Weir is Scotland's foremost writer on the outdoors. Born in Springburn, Glasgow, lives on Loch Lomondside, he is a Past President of the Scottish Mountaineering Club and Vice-President of the Scottish Rights of Way Society. He was awarded the MBE in 1976.

Simon Martin lives in St Andrews. A former journalist he spent 10 years as a salvage diver working in various wrecks round the Scottish coast.

Hugh Dougherty is a history graduate of Glasgow University, a former college lecturer and is currently press officer for education with Strathclyde Regional Council. He is a regular contributor to local and national newspapers and has a special interest in railways.

Euan McIlwraith is a radio journalist based at Aberdeen. He lives on a croft in Banffshire and collects the songs and folklore of the North-east.

Florence Tudor has always lived in Glasgow. She began her career as a soprano vocalist and entertainer on the variety stage at 15 and worked in theatres throughout Scotland.

Archie Cameron has been a poacher, gardener, chauffeur, security officer, factory manager and a camp warden. He now lives in peaceful retirement in Largs.

Maureen Reynolds was born and brought up in Dundee, but has lived at Kinloch Rannoch since 1965. She is currently working at the Exhibition Centre, Pitlochry Power Station and Dam.

Agnes Kordylewska was born and brought up in Perth. She spent 22 years in South Africa and began writing when she returned to this country and joined the Perthshire Group of the Scottish Association of Writers.

INTRODUCTION

by Maurice Fleming, Editor, *The Scots Magazine*

It has been a great pleasure to be associated with the choice of contents for this book. There were such riches at our disposal. We could, for instance, have gone right back to January 1739 and taken an extract from that very first issue. But what then? Items picked at random over the next 250 years would be of historic interest, but would not necessarily make the best reading.

We decided that we would select contents which would reflect *The Scots Magazine* of today and we have concentrated on the period 1975–1987. The one exception is Tom Weir's "Remotest North", his very first article for us, which appeared in 1949.

Our earlier years, however, are not totally neglected. Interspersed with the modern contributions are little glimpses from the past, brief extracts culled from some of the bound volumes of the long ago issues which line our office walls.

Working every day under the gaze of these venerable companions we are always conscious of the magazine's history. They remind us that we are only the latest link in a long chain reaching right back to the men who first christened and launched *The Scots Magazine*.

There were four of them, Alexander

Murray and James Cochran, who were printers, and Alexander Brymer and William Sands, booksellers.

The printing-house was in Burnet's Close, off Edinburgh's High Street, and the reasons for founding the magazine are laid out in the Preface to the January 1739 number. It speaks of the success of the *Gentleman's Magazine* and the *London Magazine* and makes the case for a new journal to cover Scottish affairs and opinion.

It promises to give readers an impartial view of political disputes, to provide news of "the occurrences of Europe", and to encourage "the Caledonian Muse". (I hope we still do!) Finally, in those times of slow and costly transport, it states that *The Scots Magazine* will be supplied "sooner and cheaper" than its London competitors.

The quickness was important, for topical news from Europe features prominently in the early copies as did births, deaths and marriages.

In addition there were essays, poems and, from July 1739, a "Journal of the Proceedings and Debates in the Political Club" – an account of recent Parliamentary debates and speeches.

As *The Scots Magazine* gained popularity it attracted contributions from some of the key figures of our national literature: Allan Ramsay, James "Ossian" Macpherson, James Boswell, Henry Mackenzie and James Hogg, who complained bitterly to Sir Walter Scott after Archibald Constable had taken over the magazine, "I have written

This dramatic illustration appeared from 1924 until monochrome photographs were introduced in the mid-1930's, when the advert and drawing moved to the back cover.

Edinburgh from The Garden

The Royal Botanic Garden (See page 353)

This was a monochrome photo and typical of those used between the mid-1930's and mid-1940's.

Magazine until 1888 when it was revived in Perth as the new title of an existing magazine, *The Scottish Church*. Much of the material now dealt with religious and moral matters, but there were pieces of general interest as well.

This period lasted until 1900 when the magazine again lapsed, not reappearing until 1924 when, owned by the St. Andrew's Society (Glasgow), it was the official organ of Scottish Societies overseas.

The modern history of *The Scots Magazine* really dates from 1927 when it passed into the hands of John Leng and Co. Ltd., and D. C. Thomson and Co. Ltd. of Dundee. J. B. Salmond was appointed Editor. An author of distinction he saw the magazine as a sort of literary review. Where, earlier, it had attracted the great writers of the 18th and 19th centuries, now it carried names such as Neil Gunn, Lewis Spence, Wendy Wood, Lewis Grassic Gibbon, George Blake and Alasdair Alpin MacGregor. These are still household names and there were many others like them in the issues of Salmond's era, making it a rich field for the literary student.

It was Salmond's successor, Arthur Daw, who successfully widened the scope of the magazine, broadening its appeal and dramatically increasing its circulation to a realistic level. He had a keen eye for up and coming writers with the popular touch and he gathered around him a strong team of contributors: Alastair Carmichael, with his humorous Highland "Oldest Boatman" stories, David Phillips, who wrote so nostalgically and memorably of old Dundee,

twice to Mr Constable, but he takes no heed of my letters, neither will he send me the *Magazine*. . . I wished to hear from him concerning the ballads which I termed 'The Mountain Bard', but he sent me no answer." I hope we do better by our contributors today.

Dilatory with his correspondence though he may sometimes have been, Constable did publish nearly 40 songs, poems and other pieces by Hogg.

In 1826 Constable's publishing business suffered in the famous financial debacle which ruined Sir Walter Scott. This disaster brought a temporary end to *The Scots*

This was a colour photo linked with a photography feature on the capital. The idea of using the cover picture to promote the contents came about when the magazine was redesigned in May 1987.

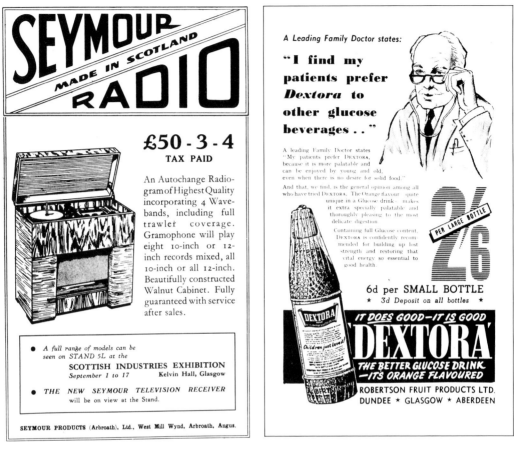
September 1949

October 1959

Campbell Finlay of Mull, the urbane Hilton Brown, novelists Nigel Tranter and Stewart Hunter, and, still writing his regular "My Month" series after a remarkable 33 years, climber and naturalist, Tom Weir. My apologies if I have omitted your own personal favourites.

Some of the writers whose work is represented in this book have been regular contributors to our pages for many years. Archie McKerracher, Rennie McOwan and John MacLeay all enjoy a strong following among *Scots Magazine* readers. There are other names here which have appeared only once or twice, but then the magazine is like that – an ever open door to writers new or established. Uppermost in our minds in making this selection was our wish to convey the range and the quality of a typical monthly issue.

No magazine ever stands still. If it does it dies on the spot. In recent years there have been many new names, new features, new ideas. There has been technological advance, too, with greatly improved colour printing facilities. *The Scots Magazine* has

September 1968

July 1979

been very much a part of the 1980's publishing scene and enters the 1990's old in experience, but young in heart.

The publication of this book marks the culmination of a year of celebrations to mark our 250th anniversary. We do hope you will enjoy it as much as we have enjoyed putting it together.

Over the years, advertisements have been a regular feature of the magazine. The ones shown here are a selection from the past

Bank Street,
Dundee.
October 1989.

[15]

WHAT THEY READ THEN

COMMON SENSE
FATAL CONSEQUENCES OF LICENTIOUSNESS IN A GOVERNMENT

It is an imputation most injurious to mankind (though it has gained too much credit in the world), that their natural disposition is apt to incline them to a distrust and dislike of those who govern them. For my own part, I am satisfied the contrary is so evident, that it has been always easy to discern in people a kind of bigotry (if I may use the expression) in favour of such as have been placed in power over them; which could not, where they have not met with more than ordinary ill usage, be got the better of: nor can I think it less than great arrogance, and a high insolence offered to mankind, to affirm, that the submission which all the civilised part of the world have thought fit to pay to governments, of one kind or another, when employed in their protection, is wholly owing to fear or the crafty management of a few individuals.

I know of few histories into which I have ever looked that have not furnished me with sufficient grounds to confirm me in my opinion; and when I have read the accounts, which the history of most countries has produced, of the barbarities, the enormous lust, the Scottish and pusillanimous indolence, or the mistaken and destructive ambition, the wanton cruelties of tyrants; the perfidiousness, the rapaciousness, the insolence of their creatures and ministers, I have had, as I thought, reason to be astonished at the insensibility of those who suffered them, who seemed to forget they were men, and could so long delay doing that justice, they owed themselves, their country, and the whole world.

Were I to look back into our own history, and that perhaps not very far, I should not want examples of the partiality people entertain towards those in the highest and most eminent stations, which has inclined them to/ acquiesce in the worst treatment, even when they have been most visibly sensible of it: but as instances of this kind may, to some, appear invidious, I will not particularise any here.

I shall therefore beg leave to consider a little the behaviour of the Romans, as they were more at liberty than most modern nations, to discover the propensity of their natural temper and sentiments, by their actions; and as they are looked upon by many (though undeservedly) as delighting in discord and tumult, and always restless and factious against their superiors. But whoever will, with accuracy and judgement, observe their conduct, will find, that though they were strenuous and violent in asserting their libery, against a most oppressive, insolent, and tyranical Nobility; yet, as their complaints were for the most part just, and their desires reasonable for a free and deserving people, they always shewed the greatest moderation in the use they made of any acquisition they gained from the Nobility in security of their liberty.

From *The Scots Magazine*, May 1739.

HUMOUR

OUR VANISHING WORDLIFE

John MacLeay

Those who know my articles in *The Scots Magazine* will be aware that unless I'm in a mood for mischief (a not infrequent frame of mind, I admit), I generally try not to confuse or in any way bamboozle those ignorant of the finer nuances of our native speech with what scholars and perhaps a few disdainful English folk style "Scotticisms". In that respect I'm like Para Handy's second-in-command who, it is averred, would never hurt anyone's feelings unless he so intended.

A Scotticism (the word suggests a witticism delivered in a Caledonian accent which admittedly is often the case) isn't necessarily a prickly, tongue-torturing word allowing only the loosest of translations: it may simply involve a peculiar, possibly eccentric grouping of otherwise familiar terms.

In the past I have stitched together a list of words and phrases that I hear all too rarely and suspect now to be imperilled beyond any conservation measures—aye, that word again. Not so far back it looked like a mispelling of "conversation", but the two words have this association: while the television (variously known as the "boax" or "choob") may have killed one, it has made the other a vital priority. Not that the telly is the only menace to our once rich and varied wordlife: other destructive influences are at work.

When I was wee, which in my own case doesn't simply mean young, but a smout or smee-yowt as I have seen it written, I and others of similarly diminutive build were likely to be hailed as, "Ha'penny face". Is anyone today? I doubt it, for now we merely have the single penny coin which doesn't have much of a ring to it. Nor, it goes without saying, much of the value, for in the halcyon days to which I refer, that coin purchased your afternoon school milk, a lunchtime tram ride or a stick of liquorice (plain liquorice as opposed to sugarolly, much fancier fare), No, there are no Ha'-penny-faces around today since we adopted that new coinage. Decimalisation is decimating our dialect.

Despite my efforts to avoid confusing English neighbours I have retained a few turns of phrase that seem apt in a given set of circumstances although I recognise this as a subconscious attempt to redress this shaky conservation balance. I still talk, for example, of the forenoon which strikes me as logical when some of those who stare blankly at me fully understand when I mention the afternoon.

Even encountered for the first time, "forenoon", it seems to me, is self-explanatory, but, alas, south of Cheviot they seem only to have mornings which we can perhaps put down to mere national differences. There is, though, in Scotland anyway, a marked difference between fore-

endangered and the "Coffee Forenoon" might just haul it back from the brink of extinction. This, apart from a potential novelty value, might serve to keep the forenoon in the foreground so to speak.

The back-end is another that has stuck with me and loosely it implies the autumn which in kindlier years may extend from late August to November. I've found the back-end coming to the fore when gardening or farming matters are in dispute. "Best to transplant in the back-end," I've suggested which has tended to sound as though I'm proposing an alternative location and I confess to seeing the scope for confusion there for I have heard the term differently applied when someone found himself playing the nether section of the comic horse in pantomine.

Meanings, if not always the words themselves, tend to alter. Not so long ago if you enquired of someone after his wife's well-being, it would have been in order to ask "How's the Mustress?" Try that today, and if it doesn't fetch you a skyte on the lug it may fetch the husband a few sour—or possibly envious—glances.

Similarly, a lady alluding to her husband would blithely have spoken of "Mah man". Today she would be thought to be referring to someone other than her spouse. Lurid newspapers and the telly have seen to that. Such a woman would at one time have run the risk of being "the talk o the steamie", but the invasion of our homes by the spin-dryer and the like have negated the threat of social ostracism at the public wash-house.

Those of us regarded as conservationists, sentimentalists, reactionaries or just plain thrawn must be only too keenly aware of the onslaught on our once-familiar speech patterns by that one-eyed monster, glowering like a malignant Cyclops from some dark corner. Through this the advertising

noon and morning, the demarcation line falling, I suppose, around ten o'clock after which it becomes acceptable to make a social or business call.

Bump into a neighbour or even, say, the insurance man and you're quite likely to advise either of them to stop by in the forenoon. Prior to the forenoon the only callers are liable to be polismen, and in the morning proper there are weans to be shunted off to school, dishes to be redd away and the like.

I suppose that first half of the day could be further sub-divided into smaa oors, morning and forenoon, but accepting my definition of the forenoon, my most recent sojourn on my old stomping ground gave me cause for anxiety. Some good ladies, socially active on behalf of worthy causes, invited me to a coffee morning which they explained would not interfere with the day's other engagements since it would be in the forenoon. Why could they not have advertised a coffee forenoon? The term, like so many others, may well be

industry has made inroads on our language.

Kids today are off-colour or pale rather than "peelie-wally". You never hear the voice-over on telly asking, "Are you peelie-wally?" It may ask whether you are listless or fatigued, but it never suggests you might be "wabbit". Let's imagine some occurrence or something that you've eaten has left you nauseous, bilious or with acid indigestion, all permissible terms to the pill and potion purveyors. A while back you might have been plain scunnered and left it at that, but the dark brown voice extolling the qualities of some cure-all could never bring itself to utter a graphic word like "scunner". Nor would the ad-men and copy-writers go overboard about it.

I referred to someone being peelie-wally, but wally too had other connotations. Wally could mean china (the substance that is, not the country) as in wally dugs, those mournful canines of indeterminate breed who generally guarded the marble clocks on old-fashioned mantelpieces. Now that their value has increased, they are Staffordshire china dogs as I learned from a television programme about antiques.

Wally, though, in the plural had a further meaning. Should my father lament at the table that his dentures marred his enjoyment of the meal, my mother might, with a wink at me, make one of her rare lapses into the vernacular: "That's the grand thing aboot havin your ain wallies." Yes, wallies were teeth, but can you imagine one of those telly-ad dentists advising us to use a specific toothpaste guaranteed to make our wallies glisten?

Just as wallies seem to have bitten the dust along with other things, so many other terms must have perished. Let's face it, the advertising men can just about swing a toilet preparation as capable of imparting "under arm charm", but I fail to see how they could weave an effective fantasy around the "oxter" as the armpit was of old. Legend has it that one briefly-considered slogan ran, "Let your armpits be charmpits" which allows at least a McGonagallian rhyme, but oxter—? I can't come up with a possible rhyme short of "jokester" which, however neatly it may be made to scan, isn't likely to sell many aerosols.

No, perhaps we had better accept that the oxter is, as at least one poet phrased it, "for the pipes" and let that fly stick to the waa as the saying has it—or rather, had it—for these days we can't let flies remain stuck to waas as the set reminds us, showing us a lethal press-button device seemingly capable of immobilising a kamikaze pilot, designed to ensure that no flies stay stuck anywhere.

Before leaving the humble oxter (which to most youngsters these days probably sounds like an endangered bovine) I must give way to a stray thought. I still recall folk being "up tae the oxters" in work, trouble or debt. Today, many who would once have settled for being oxter-deep in financial difficulties talk of being mortgaged up to the hilt. A little hackneyed, you'll allow, but perhaps we could let our Scots logic and individuality prevail here so that any Scotsman finding himself only knee-deep in debt could go the whole hog adding that he's mortgaged up to the *kilt*.

By adapting this sort of cliché we are establishing some redress and I made one youthful contribution in this airt by describing a wee lassie fair carried away by her game of peevers as being at "peever pitch".

We see, though, that while advertising may never have intended any direct assault on our speech idioms it has made survival difficult for some words. Whether the voice-over on the telly is enthusing over some perfumed soap or a cleaning agent,

[19]

the lyrical descriptions, the revered tones, rule out the remotest possibility of the products being used in association with, let alone poured into, a humble "jawbox".

The dreamy-voiced mother urging the youngster to test the alleged properties of the washing-up liquid could scarcely turn around and order the wean to "stop skiddlin at wunst". "Skiddlin" was something bairns of previous generations did around sink, bowl, wash-basin, tin bath, galvie bucket or any other receptacle filled with water. It involved any use of this fluid (largely scooshin or scootin) short of actually washing, an activity that child psychologists might deign creative play, for the average wean could find in any container of water more possibilities than Gavin Maxwell's otters ever did.

Mothers in floral peenies, grannies with arms flourcoated to their dimpled elbows regarded it as mere skiddlin likely to result in mess and therefore to be discouraged. Any telly mum egging the kid on to swirl the water around, blow bubbles, etc., would lose an awful lot of face by letting patience fray and skelloching out, "Stop yon skiddlin!" True, telly mothers do not skelloch or skirl, but, och, it's a sair look out for skiddlin right enough.

I used to feel that I was likely to sustain a literal loss of face through "slunging" it, an operation consisting of liberally splashing cold water on to the countenance to clear it of excess soap. "Mind an slunge yer face," my granny would jog my memory and perhaps a sluggish elbow.

Slunging, you see, was guaranteed to bring a glow to the cheeks, a flush that owed much to loss of breath. Today's soaps, being, as they are, permeated with exotic oils, perfumes, perhaps the elixir of youth itself, it would be almost sacrilegious to merely slunge away these magical substances. Slunging itself seems destined to

go spiralling down that plug-hole, which today may suffer from blockage, but never through being "stappit".

We have today a Trade Descriptions Act putting a curb if not the branks on the excessive claims dreamed up by the ad-poets, which means that our far-famed (sometimes far-flung) native breakfast dish cannot be promoted in the same way as our parents pushed it at—and occasionally down—us. We will never see flashed across our screens such claims as, "MacWhangle's Oatmeal—the breakfast that pits hairs on yer chist" or "Sprott's Porridge—it sticks tae yer ribs". Unless that is, extensive medical research reveals that such things do come about consequent to the consumption of porridge.

Not too long ago, although it is too long to recall with complacency, I was vainly trying to impress upon my daughter the advantages of porridge over the fancier

" Mind an slunge yer face!"

packaged breakfast soggies. I was prepared to compromise my principles to a
point by permitting her to take sugar in the
English manner as opposed to the gourmet
approach favoured by ourselves: after all
I'd hate to be thought racist. I took care to
avoid the exhortations that had assailed my
childish lug: "Eat it up, it'll pit herrs oan yer
chist", a prospect which had horrified me
let alone my sisters. At the age of six I had
no wish to display a hirsute thorax when no
other wean in the school did. However, I
fell into the trap of telling my daughter that
it would stick to her ribs.

It seemed the appropriate thing at the
time, but it does present a somewhat
unappealing image. What youngsters
worth their salt (that's assuming they take
their porridge in the approved Scots manner) want rib cages clogged with tepid
brose?

Sadly, my daughter, who is half-English
anyway—but then nobody's perfect—
struck porridge off her staple diet forever
despite my warnings, "Ye'll never be a big
strong man like your mother.'

The pet food manufacturers, too, have a
few sins to answer for. To be sure they
have gone to great lengths to create a
balanced diet for Puss or Pussy, but what
about Cheetie? Have they exterminated for
good and all that once familiar family feline
that coiled before the fire ready to trip up
the unwary carrier of a tea tray? I could
pedantically point out that "Puss" tradi-
tionally in Scotland was the hare, but not
wanting to be accused of hare-splitting I'll
get back to the Cheetie cat. Pussy cats
belong in story books (usually in thigh-
length boots) but our battling terrors of the
middens were Cheetie cats and moreover
they knew it for they came running if so
addressed: "Here, Cheetie!"

Now, you've never heard a cat breeder
(who looks and sounds suspiciously like an

actor) tell you that Cheetie will benefit from
eating Fishkas or whatever. No, they've
killed off our cheetie and gone in for
pussies.

That name though, Cheetie: how did it
come about? It could be derived from
cheetah, hardly the most familiar of the cat
tribe in Scotland. Or should it be spelled
"Cheatie"? That would seem reasonable,
bearing in mind some of the devious,
sleekit near-Machiavellian creatures I have
kept.

At least tewkie or chookie as in "tewkie
burdie" is fairly self-explanatory although
I've never made accurate identification of
the particular one that in the Glasgow
rhyme "laid an egg on the windae sole". I
imagine that sole should be "sill" but it had
to rhyme with the "tol-lol-lol" in the earlier
line. Now we've had adverts pushing stuff
at us that makes budgies stot—sorry—
bounce and canaries cheep (indeed the best
time to buy them is when they are going
"cheep") but where's tewkie burdie's cut of
all this avian action? Perhaps I am unfair:
maybe that tewkie in the rhyme was the
last of the line, the final egg and the entire
species doomed when "the windae sole
began to crack".

One thing television has done is to give
all breeds of dog a crack of the whip—well,
the leash anyway. In bygone years a "dug",
to be accepted as such, had to stand at least
waist-high and be capable of "tearin the
heid aff" any other canine. Anything else
belonged stuck in the middle of a postcard
near asphyxiation point from a garotte of
tartan ribbon. These were scathingly dis-
missed as "poatlickers" and their presence
prompted questions like:

"Caa yon a dug? Whidye use it fur?
Waashin the windaes?"

"Did ye knit it yersel? Ah think ye
drapped a few stitches!"

Alas, it's farewell to poatlickers, haunknittit dugs and cheeties.

It's so long since a cat was addressed as "Cheetie" that it probably wouldn't even recognise its own name. You don't believe me? Well, I put my theory to the test and with no success. I was totally ignored.

I supposed they must have been English cheeties.

FITBA DAFT!

Bob Morrow

Like thousands of fellow Scots, I have had a go at the fitba. "Had a go" pretty well sums it up, because I freely admit I didn't make much of it. Still, you learn something from everything, and as a boy of ten, football introduced me to the joyous exhilaration which can be part of the state of being mucky, filthy dirty.

This came with my debut for the school team. After a week of non-stop visits to admire my name on the notice board, I was handed my jersey and pants, and rushed home, where my mother washed and ironed them lovingly.

My euphoria lasted right up to the Saturday morning and our arrival in the shadow of the Campsie Fells, where the match was to be played. I ran out eagerly in my spotless kit and saw a muddy no-man's-land of baby puddles, mammy puddles, and whacking big daddy puddles.

I was appalled. I didn't know the meaning of the word then, but that's what I was, and for the first quarter of an hour, I tip-toed around trying miserably to find dry land. Then one of the other team unsportingly sent me sprawling full length into the biggest of the wee lochs. I spluttered to my feet, mud and water dripping off me. Then, realisation dawned that I was now immune.

I couldn't possibly get any wetter or dirtier, and from that moment I was transformed. I charged through the deepest puddles with carefree abandon. I think I even scored a goal at the shallow end, which I hoped would mollify my mother. It didn't.

What strikes me now is the fact that the teacher who gave up his Saturdays to lug us around, must have been as drookit as the rest of us. He was one of the host of dedicated men and women who give freely of their time and money, to run the teams from schools, Boys' Brigade, Under-age Leagues, and juniors.

Why they do it I don't know. I reckon they must simply be good people. One such character is "Just call me Wullie" McAdam, self-appointed manager, trainer, and second father, to a boys' team, Auchinvale Thistle, in Stirlingshire. Friday night starts his worries. That's when Wullie listens keenly to the weather forecast. If it's for heavy rain, then he knows he'll need to be at the park early with buckets and brushes to clear the worst parts.

That done, he goes home for breakfast, then starts to ferry some of the team in his car, trusting that the parents of his other would-be stars will do likewise. Admitting reluctantly that it costs him roughly £15 per week, mostly for petrol, he says "Och, well, it's worth it. The lads depend on me, and I manage fine." Cackling with laughter, he adds, "If you don't count the Saturday we turned up to find somebody had stolen the goal-posts!"

A good example of Wullie's trials and tribulations would be the day when he traipsed his team to Edinburgh to play a cup-tie. There the referee informed him that he had decided to call off the game because of the state of the ground. After consultation with his opposition counter-part, Wullie intimated to the official that both teams were quite willing to go ahead with the match. The referee's response was brief and to the point. "The game's off and that's that."

Wullie, a bit huffy, and thinking of the wasted journey, asked, "What's up then? Are you in a hurry to get your Christmas shopping done?"

This brought a stern warning to give less of his cheek or he would be reported, and Wullie, well aware that his share of the minibus was already £20, held his tongue and silently nursed his wrath all the way home.

The first of these selfless characters I remember was Old Joe Martin, who ran an impecunious junior team in Kilsyth. Called Kilsyth Emmett, it is now long defunct. Joe picked the team, repaired the boots and nets, packed the hamper, and cut the grass. He blew up the ball, lined the park with sawdust, and acted as linesman during games, somehow finding the time between all these chores to mend the holes in the fence through which we kids crawled on Saturday afternoons. As extras, he dished out bus fares to players when necessary, and bought them fish suppers after the game. The money came from slaving six and a half days down the pit.

Enthusiast is hardly the word for men like Joe, and Mrs Joe, not to be outdone, washed the jerseys, pants and stockings, and darned them when needed, which was pretty much all the time.

Quite apart from all that, I could never forget Joe for one piece of immortal advice. It came just before his team took the field to face a side renowned for their physical attributes. Asked anxiously by one of his younger players, "If they start kickin us, wull we retaliate?", Old Joe looked at the lad for a moment, then delivered the following gem, "Ah think, wi this lot son, you'd be as weel tae retaliate first!"

Often on Saturdays, Joe would go straight from the pit to the park, as did half his team. The wooden hut which served as a clubhouse had nothing even remotely resembling a bath, so they played as they were—covered in coal dust from head to foot. Such conditions were commonplace in mining areas until not so very long ago, and no one thought anything of it. Only when these athletic apparitions appeared in the bigger towns was any comment aroused.

I can remember a cup final played at Brockville Park in Falkirk, where most of the participants were of a decidedly dusky hue, but it was the goalkeeper of the Fife team who intrigued the neutrals. Straight

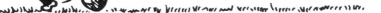

from what must have been the dirtiest section of the pit, he was as black as night, and all that could be seen were two white eyes. He was immediately christened Al Jolson, and played with the choruses of "Mammy" and "Swanee" filling the air behind him. Now try to imagine how they looked after half an hour's sweaty exertion on a hot summer's day. For all the world like a tribe of war-painted Red Indians!

Wullie McAdam admits he has never seen the coal dust brigade, but says with a smile, "Nothing would surprise me in the football basement. I've had a goalkeeper with earplugs, listening enraptured to his transistor as the ball went flashing past.

"I've got a really good wee player now" he continues, "but he's a jeely piece addict. Goes through four or five per game. I've got used to seeing him coming through with the ball, his face all raspberry jam."

One ex-player I talked to remembered best of all a cup-tie he played in Lanarkshire. "It was one of those wee villages where the miners' rows bordered the touchline," he recalled with a chuckle. "I was having a great game. I scored two goals in the first half-hour, and the home supporters were beginning to shout, 'You'll need to stop that yin.' Well, if they didn't exactly stop me, they certainly slowed me doon." I waited. "I was taking a throw-in," he grinned, "and a woman hit me over the head with a frying pan!"

This stalwart, Peter Martin, now devotes his time to a young lads' team. He laughed when I told him the story of the corner kick that never was. This happened years ago in an evening juvenile game where one player found he suddenly had to call off. He kindly offered the use of his footwear to his bootless deputy. Unfortunately, a size 11 on a size 8 foot is contrary to Nature's intention, but the difference was made up with the liberal use of newspaper.

Jock, the slightly-built deputy, did his heroic best, ignoring loud and pointed references to his Mickey Mouse feet, but as the game progressed, his side of the field gradually became littered with scraps of newsprint.

The climax came in the last few minutes when, well into the gloaming, Jock's team were awarded a corner kick. Desperate for a late score, they waited tense with anticipation in the goalmouth. With cries of, "C'mon, Jock," urging him on, he took a wild swipe at the ball. What came sailing through the gloom to be despatched into the net, was not the ball, but—you've guessed—an oversize boot.

The referee immediately awarded a goal and headed for the centre circle with the outraged goalkeeper in pursuit brandishing the offending footwear. While all this stushie was going on, Jock, with commendable acumen, sneaked across and tapped the ball into the back of his opponents' net, thus giving the referee justification for letting the goal stand.

Peter Martin just couldn't let that past him. "Wait till I tell you about McAllister," he smiled. "He was one of my youth club players. A good defender he was, and a snooker expert, too. Well, he had his head shaved for one of these sponsored things, and on the first hairless match he played, he went up to head a ball clear and it skidded off into his own net. Somebody shouted, 'For ony sake, McAllister—chalk yer cue!'"

I asked him what makes a man give up so much of his time for no tangible reward. "Maybe I'm just daft," he grinned. "A lot of Saturdays I've stood there, the rain streaming down my neck, and promised myself this would be my last season. Then when my mind's about made up, along comes a new wee hopeful with the old request, 'Can I get a game fur your team, Mr Martin, sur?' and I'm off again."

Jock tapped the ball into the net while the goalkeeper protested to the referee.

I have kept my favourite football story to the last, because it concerns a game in which I took part. Early in 1942, my army unit was sent to the Sudan, and on our arrival, we were immediately challenged by the local village team. They turned out like liquorice all-sorts, in a variety of jerseys, and all in their bare feet. Shed no tears for them, however, for they had pedal extremities like Aberdeen granite, as we very soon discovered. We played a number of games against them, and at the end of our sojourn, the District Commissioner asked our Colonel if the last match could be played on their field, and with their referee. To this the Colonel happily agreed, and we duly set off to the arena, a sandy waste in the middle of a complex of mud huts.

Urged on by 2000 Souks all banging spears on huge hide shields, the local team set about us, intent on victory. As the game progressed, the clamour mounted. With donkeys braying excitedly, and camels roaring, we doggedly defended the honour of Scotland.

With the score still at nil-nil, the moment to savour came ten minutes from time. Jimmy Clunie, our centre-forward, latched on to a long clearance, dribbled round a donkey which had wandered on to the field, circumnavigated a camel that had followed it, and lashed the ball into the back of the Sudanese net. Instantly, our celebrations were nipped in the bud by the referee, who not only discounted the goal, but gave a foul against Clunie, presumably for jostling the donkey.

To add insult to injury, and with time running out, he then, with Arabian aplomb, awarded a penalty kick to his tribesmen. It was an outrageous decision, but we as a team, had unanimously and silently decided to let prudence prevail, and we kept quiet. Alex Mutch, our Aberdeenshire goalkeeper, had the situation summed up. Resignation all over his face, he said to me, "Just let him kick it into goal. Ah'll move oot the road!"

I have had this ongoing love affair with the game of football since I could toddle, but it seems an eternity since I went around knocking doors with other wee hopefuls, presenting our grubby petition to harassed housewives. It read:

Please help our little football team,
It is so very small,
But every ha'penny that you give,
Will help to buy a ball.

Looking back, I don't think that we ever got enough to buy a ball, but I seem to remember the Lucky Bags and the Conversation Lozenges ∎

WHAT THEY READ THEN

TO THE AUTHOR OF *THE SCOTS MAGAZINE*

Westminster July 9

Sir,

Your countrymen cannot be too frequently reminded of the importance of an increase in their attention to Trade, and especially those branches for which your clime and situation are more peculiarly fitted; in which respect the improvement of your Fishery in general, which I just mentioned in my last, deserves the consideration of every man who would rejoice at the increase of the wealth and prosperity of Scotland.

If the soil in some parts of your country be not so fertile as what your neighbours enjoy, nature has, for the most part, supplied the defect, by an opportunity of making that wealth abound near the most barren cliffs, which more inland countries can never hope for; and the most neglected shore in the worst of your country is fitter for the purpose of curing and drying fish, net-making etc. then any the Dutch have to boast of; who yet, by the help of indefatigable industry, supply every deficiency of their country, and upon ice, and in floats contrived for that purpose, execute the greatest part of their business in preparations, and etc. for their Fisheries; and their vessels are glad, under numerous difficulties, to cure most, and even dry some of their fish; while your shores would answer all those ends, and many more; and one boy might, with great ease, turn and attend more fish upon the side of a sea-bank, then by the help of six men could be done in the same time on board a ship.

Salt so essential an article in this business, you have an opportunity of making in several parts of your coast, at the smallest expense; and labour is so cheap in the places fittest for carrying on an extensive fishery, as to render reasonable a prospect of pursuing that beneficial branch of commerce, at a more moderate expense than has yet been anywhere practised, or, indeed, than can be done in any other country. Particular instructions for the execution of this useful work, this easy, plain road to riches, I shall not, at present, offer you; in hope that some of the Gentlemen who are most nearly interested in the success of such undertakings, will assist the public with the necessary computations, and whatever else relates to so general a benefit: for in a case of so public a nature, where all must reap a proportion of the advantage, all ought to consider themselves equally interested in so desirable an improvement; so that to withhold any assistance from such a design, would be denying your country that endeavour to serve her which every man owes the place of his birth. And as an affair of such moment will bear, and in some measure require repetition; you may, I believe, without danger of disobliging your readers, insert whatever you receive upon a subject in which they must see themselves so nearly concerned.

From *The Scots Magazine*, 1739.

WILDLIFE

UP AT THE MARTENS'

West Highland naturalist **Lea MacNally** investigates the feeding habits of one of our rarest and most beautiful animals.

Crouched uncomfortably behind a huge slab of Torridonian sandstone, a grey cloud of insatiable midges feasting on my face, I was at the stage of debating whether I was quite sane. It was a dull, damp evening in early September and I was waiting hopefully for a pine marten. Ahead of me, 50 yards away, squeezed in between rocks almost as tall as itself, was a large rowan tree, more vermilion than green so abundant were its clusters of berries. It was to these, I felt sure, that a pine marten would be coming. What I was not sure of was whether it would be before or after dark. Hence my midge-tormented vigil.

You may well wonder why I thought that a member of the predatory *mustelidae*, even a tree-climbing one like the pine marten, would be interested in rowan berries. The pine marten, however, while primarily a meat-eating predator, is as omnivorous as the badger and has a very definite taste for berries. Raspberries, blackcurrants, and blaeberries are all eaten in season, and as most humans also relish these it seems understandable. But rowan berries?

While edible at a pinch, rowans are certainly not enjoyed by humans. Nevertheless, I had suspected the consumption of rowan berries to be a seasonal habit of martens in the North-west, for every year

I've found little clusters of what were obviously semi-digested, then regurgitated, rowan berries in rocky places which are the haunt of these animals. When I found a substantial number of these regurgitated berries, some of them alongside pine marten droppings—the trail had led me to this rowan tree.

※　　※　　※

Before my vigil, I had taken the precaution of daubing myself with anti-midge cream and it was just as well. When I reached the tree, about 7 p.m., there didn't seem to be a midge around, but hardly had I settled down on the damp moss when they began to orbit madly around my head. After a long five minutes had elapsed, I was peering through a grey net curtain of them, a curtain which bit as well as obscured!

Discomfort was forgotten though, when, at 7.20, a flicker of dark fur darted over a rock near the base of the rowan. A pine marten! It flashed up the smooth grey trunk and became completely hidden among the thick foliage, only a periodic shaking of the leaves indicating its presence. My 8 × 30 glasses, hard to hold still in my excitement, now and then revealed tantalising glimpses of the marten as it plundered the ripe berries. Now and again, too, I saw the bushy tail hanging straight down, all else hidden.

Suddenly the marten came into magnificent view as it emerged on to the outer edge of the tree's canopy. It seemed incredible that these slender twigs could support the weight. It was a most handsome young marten, with dark brown glossy fur and a rich orange-yellow frontlet. I could now absorb the sight of the graceful wee animal, at home in the tree as any squirrel. The method of eating was to cling with all four paws and stretch up to the berries above, the muzzle disclosing sharp, white teeth. Occasionally a front paw was used to steady the fruit while the jaws snipped busily.

For perhaps two minutes I watched, utterly fascinated by the beautiful picture: green foliage ablaze with berries, and the glowing orange-chested pine marten for a centre piece. How I wished I was within camera range.

Suddenly the noisy scolding call from one of a family of ring ouzels, sharing the berries, sent the lithe little animal scurrying head-first down the trunk and into the rocks. However, realising almost at once that it was a false alarm, the marten was back up the tree in seconds. The ring ouzels were in dangerous company for, below the tree, a scattering of dusky black-brown feathers testified that their dining companion was not interested exclusively in the berries.

I tried hard to forget the swarming midges, but now I was even breathing them in. So thick was the cloud around my head that at one point I thought the marten could not fail to notice me.

All movement ceased for some minutes. Was feeding over or was it continuing on the far side of the tree? I anointed myself anew with anti-midge cream, gritted my teeth and decided to give it another few

The pine marten is an alert and vivacious little creature and a pleasure to watch as Lea MacNally relates here.   PHOTO: LEA MACNALLY

minutes. My reward came quickly. A sinuous body emerged, instantly followed by a twin. There were two! I watched entranced as they had a playful tussle at the foot of the tree, then one sprang to a vantage point on the trunk and a game of king of the castle ensued. They were in the upper leaves, but breaks in the greenery allowed me brief sightings as they fed together. A moment or so later came the highlight of my watch, when both martens came out on to the outer edge of the tree. A memorable sight! Their orange frontlets gleaming, pointed heads turning this way and that, they rapidly snipped off berries with their glistening teeth.

After a few blissful moments, with the midges forgotten, I watched both martens disappear inwards and the tree was still. I peered at my watch and saw it was 8 p.m. Little wonder the light was fading. Reluctant to go, I lingered for another few minutes, to reap a final reward as I glimpsed a marten scurrying uphill, using an enormous horizontal slab of sandstone to avoid the jungle of tall heather surrounding the rocks. These wee animals seldom seem to move except at top speed.

I left as the first bat of the evening flitted above my head. I had been more fortunate than I'd appreciated that first night, for though I was to watch on many future occasions, I never again saw both martens together. The tree continued to be visited, and berries eaten, until, by mid-October, the crop was gone. The regurgitated clusters were everywhere, even in the hide I'd erected to take photographs.

❏   ❏   ❏

I put out bait in the shape of little squares of bread and jam, and the first night I did this

After all the activity observed by the writer it's not surprising that this one is tired.

PHOTO: LEA MACNALLY

[29]

the marten came to feed while I crouched in my hide with camera ready. It took much patience, many visits and many disappointments, but I did get some worthwhile photographs.

The marten always came like a wraith, apparently materialising from a jumble of rocks. It would pause for a second or two as it tested the air, muzzle upwards, and finally, with a lithe bound come over to the bait. After watching it devour every vestige of jam from the bread, I tried jam alone on subsequent occasions, raspberry if possible for this seemed a first choice. I discount, however, the assertion of a friend, who'd fed martens at his bird table, that they had a distinct preference for Hartley's!

The sweet bait alone proved most effective, and on one occasion, even a piece of jam-soaked moss was carried off by the marten. An almost full 1 lb jar of raspberry which I'd left lidless, but hidden, and securely wrapped (so I thought) and stuck into a crack at the top of a large rock, was plundered of its entire contents in a night. I dealt with this problem by ensuring thereafter that the jar always had a proper lid screwed on tight.

I tried an egg one night and the marten sniffed uncertainly and then ignored it. The following evening it had a change of heart and carried it away. I also experimented with various fruits: brambles, elderberries, blackcurrants, apple and pear slices were all eaten; rosehips, holly berries and tomatoes were spurned. Meat of most kinds, whether raw or cooked scraps, was taken. Haggis, too, was a success as were Swiss roll, ginger cake and apple pie.

I found I was feeding some interlopers as well, two voles living dangerously as it turned out, for I later found the skull and bones of one in a marten dropping. A robin was also a regular, but the most intriguing diner of all was a diminutive weasel. Twice it visited the stone slab food table, when the menu was strong-smelling raw venison. These scraps, some longer than itself, were trailed and tugged away, with a hectic struggle when they tangled in heather.

My observations at the tree were a most worthwhile exercise and I now know, beyond all doubt, that pine martens do eat and enjoy rowan berries. What still remains to be discovered is why some of the berries are regurgitated half-digested, but that will be another story.

STRANGE THINGS

A VISION OF NECHTANESMERE

James F. McHarg

On a dark January night in 1950, a middle-aged lady, Miss E. F. Smith, was walking home to the village of Letham, in Angus, when she saw moving figures with torches. Her experience, which I investigated some years later, and reported in *The Journal of the Society for Psychical Research (Vol 49)* is, I believe, worth recording here.

Was it a vision of the aftermath of the Battle of Nechtanesmere? There are points in her story which seem to indicate that it was and it is worth noticing that there have been reports of similar experiences at other battle sites. In England there have been those at Edgehill which began only a few days after the fighting there in 1642. In Scotland, incidents reported from Culloden are probably the best known.

Miss Smith's vision—if that's what it was—was brought to my attention in 1971 by friends of mine, the late Lt. Colonel C. G. Hampton and Mrs Hampton. They, in turn, knew of it through their friends Mr and Mrs I. A. MacKnight and Miss Ruth Dundas. I was immediately interested, for as a psychiatrist, I had studied hallucinatory experiences, and as a member of the Society for Psychical Research I am interested in the truth of *some* hallucinations.

I decided I would like to meet Miss Smith and, if possible, record her description of the event since it seemed that this had never been done. Accordingly, my friends kindly arranged for me to meet her. We had a preliminary talk then and she willingly agreed for me to make a return visit with a tape-recorder. This I did on September 22nd of that year. Miss Smith was then in her 70s and her eyesight was failing. Her mind, however, was still clear and she was fit enough to come out with me and tour by car the route she had covered on foot on that night 21 years earlier.

This is the story she told me: On 2 January 1950 she had been to a cocktail party at a friend's house in Brechin, and stayed on for dinner. It was late at night when she set out for home in her car. A fall of snow had been followed by rain and, two miles outside Brechin, "just by Aldbar School," the car skidded into a ditch. There was no question of the skid having been due to a faint turn, or other lapse of consciousness, nor of Miss Smith having been injured or concussed in any way. She had to abandon her car, however, and opted to continue her journey on foot rather than return to Brechin and disturb her friends. She had still a distance of about eight miles to go. Her little dog, a poodle, was with her and for the last two miles of the journey she had to carry him on her shoulder. The walk was along deserted country roads, in a countryside with a few scattered farms.

As she neared Letham, Miss Smith must have been fairly exhausted. She must also have felt rather nervous immediately prior to the onset of the apparition for she deliberately did not take a short-cut home which would have taken her alongside a dark, wooded area.

The apparition began when she was about half a mile from the first houses of Letham village and it continued until she reached them. The time was getting on for 2 a.m. and the probable total duration of the experience I estimate at about 12 minutes.

Miss Smith was approaching a crest of the road over which, by daylight, the top of Dunnichen Hill would first have come into sight, when she saw moving torches straight ahead about a mile away. When she turned left at a T-junction the distant lights were then on her right. A little lower down the winding road on her right, about a third of a mile away, she then saw further figures carrying torches. She finally watched figures even closer to her, in the field, on the right, about 50 yards away, in the direction of some farm buildings—which were not visible in the darkness.

At this stage, the dog had started to react. Miss Smith said, "He was sitting on my left shoulder and he turned and looked at the lights and started growling and I thought, 'Now next he's going to bark.'" She said she was anxious in case her pet woke up the village.

The apparition ended when she left it behind as she entered the village through which she continued to her own home—a distance of perhaps a further quarter of a mile—where she went straight to bed. At no time had she stopped to watch, in fact she felt a positive disinclination to linger.

It had been, exclusively, something she had *seen*. There had been no preceding hallucinations of smell or taste which might have suggested a disturbance in the temporal lobes of the brain. Only on waking in the morning, she said, had she realised what a strange experience it had been. The details of what she actually saw are illus-trated by extracts from Miss Smith's account, but I will first make some comments on the rediscovery of the original site of the "mere" of Nechtan by the late Dr F. T. Wainwright, one time Head of the Department of History at Queen's College, Dundee. He had done his research only three years before Miss Smith's experience.

The name "Nechtanesmere" is not, and never has been, in use locally. It would seem to have been given to the loch by English chroniclers of the battle. The loch no longer exists and, indeed, its original site was long a matter of conjecture. A patchwork of fields, with their fences and boundaries, effectively camouflages it and, as viewed from the surrounding roads, there is now nothing to indicate its original outline or even to suggest the presence of a loch.

Dr Wainwright had noticed, in 1947, how floods following the previous winter had temporarily restored at least part of the old loch and how, in the following summer, as a result of faint changes in the grasses, the floodmarks in the fields could still be seen. He determined to try to indicate on a map the extent of the vanished loch and did so with the aid of photography and a field survey to determine contour lines.

On the basis of this survey he repro-duced an Ordnance Survey Map of the district on which he had superimposed the boundaries of the loch. This shows a finger of the loch projecting in a north-easterly direction, round which people moving towards the east would have had to detour.

It is known that the Battle of Nechtanes-mere (generally regarded, in the late 7th century, as one of the outstanding events of the age) took place on the afternoon of Saturday 20 May 685. In it the North-umbrians, under their king, Ecgfrith, were decisively beaten by the Picts, under their

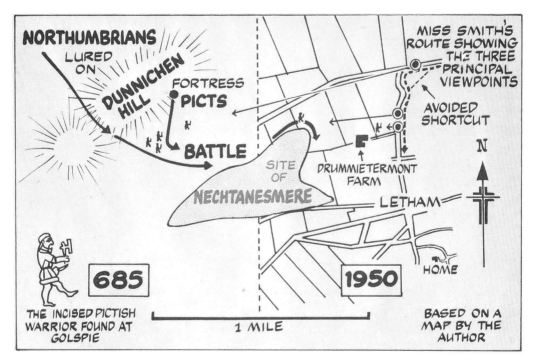

king, Brude mac Beli. The battle marked the end of an aggressive expedition by Ecgfrith undertaken against the advice of St Cuthbert and other Northumbrian notables.

Little is known for certain about the expedition prior to the battle, but it has been suggested that the Northumbrians, already in control in the Lothians, crossed the Forth near Stirling, and the Tay near Perth. Of the two alternative routes after that—south or north of the Sidlaw Hills—it is thought more probable that they took the northern route through Strathmore as far as Dunnichen Hill.

The suggestion is that Ecgfrith was there drawn off his route by a feigned Pictish retreat through the cleft in that hill and that the Northumbrians, bursting through the cleft, realised too late that a Pictish fortress on the south side, invisible from the north, lay only 300–400 yards to their left. It is presumed that, with rein-forcements from the fortress, pursuit by the Northumbrians was quickly turned into flight downhill towards the mere at the bottom.

What is certain is that Ecgfrith himself was slain and his whole royal bodyguard around him. It is reported, indeed, that most of the Northumbrian army was killed—the few who survived no doubt did so by fleeing. Ecgfrith's body, however, was carried off to the royal burial ground at Iona, where the Abbot was Adamnan, biographer of St Columba and friend both of Ecgfrith's brother and Brude mac Beli.

The activity of dealing with the dead after the battle, presumably by the Picts themselves, would no doubt have continued throughout the following night. Dr C. W. Fraser, of the Department of Astronomy at St Andrews University, told me that on 20/21 May, 685, sunset would have been about 8 p.m., and that although after 10 May in that part of Scotland it is never

c

completely dark at night it would have become relatively dark (presumably requiring torches for any serious work) from about 9.15 p.m. until about 2.30 a.m. The time of the apparition was shortly before 2 a.m.

I took daytime photographs of the landscape from different points along Miss Smith's route and also walked it in order to estimate the total duration of the apparition. In addition I visited the site on the anniversary of the battle on 20/21 May 1976 at about 2 a.m. (the time of the apparition in January 1950) in order to compare for myself the state of the light at that time of the year with the blackness of a January night.

I should make it quite clear that Miss Smith was in no sense a patient and I made no psychiatric assessment of her health. I certainly detected nothing to suggest any clinical condition.

In my recorded interview with her, Miss Smith said that when she first saw the lights straight ahead in the distance, the figures "looked as if they were carrying flaming torches . . . and there were quite a lot of torches." She had the feeling that what she was seeing had not suddenly started, but that it had already been going on when she came upon it. Her recalled reaction was to say to herself, "Well, that's an incredible thing!"

The nearer figures carrying torches which she saw later were, she said, "quite obviously skirting the mere" (which didn't exist then, of course) "because they didn't walk, from where I was looking, straight across to the far corner of the field, they *came round . . .*" Speaking about the

Eight miles from Letham is Aldbar school. It was on the road here that Miss Smith's car skidded forcing her to continue her journey home on foot.   PHOTO: JOHN RUNDLE

nearest figures of all—the last ones she watched—Miss Smith said, "They were obviously looking for their own dead . . . the one I was watching, the one nearest the roadside, would bend down and turn a body over, and if he didn't like the look of it, he just turned it back on its face and went on to the next one . . . There were several of them . . . I *supposed* they were going to bury them."

When I asked what the figures were wearing Miss Smith said, "They looked as if they were in—well, I would have said brown, but that was merely the light—anyway, dark tights, the whole way up . . . a sort of overall, with a roll-collar, and at the end of their tunics there was a larger roll round them, too. And it simply went on looking like tights until it reached their feet. I did not see what was on their feet. But there weren't long boots. . ."

This is interesting because the carving of a Pictish warrior on a stone at Golspie shows a bootless figure and gives the impression both of tights and of a roll-necked tunic with what could be a "roll" at the bottom of it.

When I asked about headgear, she said that the figures she saw were wearing " . . . the kind of thing a baker's boy used to wear . . . Just like a hard roll of material, round, stuck on the top of their heads . . . excellent for carrying things on top of the head with."

The bearded Pictish warrior on the stone appears to have long hair and no headgear.

When asked about the torches Miss Smith said " . . . they were carrying very long torches in their left hands . . . very red . . . Afterwards I wondered what on earth they'd been made of—tar, I suppose. *Was* there tar in those days?"

At the time of the interview I assumed that Miss Smith meant that the flames of the torches had been unusually red, but she may equally well have meant that it had been their shafts. Miss Ruth Dundas has given me the useful information that torches used to be made from the resinous roots of the Scots fir which, in their natural state, do indeed have a distinctive red colour and this would perhaps be stronger in torchlight.

Miss Dundas referred me to the (Old) *Statistical Account of Scotland 1791–1799* from which it is clear that such roots were still being used for lighting purposes at the end of the 18th century. This account, after referring to " . . . that immense forest of fir, which once covered the muirs of this part of the Highlands," records that "everywhere the country people dig for roots of fir, in the mosses, both for light and firewood." This extract related to the parish of Fortingall, but such roots would have been equally available at Nechtanesmere, for Dunnichen Hill was no doubt crowned then with the Scots firs of the old Caledonian Forest. If all this is so, Miss Smith's surprise at the redness of the torches may be a point of significance because her supposition that they were made of *tar* clearly indicates that she did not have any preconceived idea about them.

How is her story to be interpreted? There seem to be three basic possibilities.

Firstly, that there was no apparition at all, and the whole thing was a fraud or a hoax, and Miss Smith had been laughing up her sleeve at the attention paid by her friends to a complete fabrication.

Secondly, it is possible that again there was no apparitional experience at all, but that, without any question of a deliberate hoax, a false memory had arisen in Miss Smith's mind on the following morning, the content of which could have been based upon mere musings she could have had the previous night while passing the site of the ancient battle. On this supposition one might speculate whether, had she met a friend on that road, she would have actually commented on the strange scene, and whether the little dog really did see, and growl at, the torches, and not just at a rat or a rabbit he had noticed in the hedgerow.

Thirdly, it is possible, and perhaps most probable, that she did have the series of visual experiences essentially as she described it.

If the apparition really did occur, it seems likely that Miss Smith had been in an "altered" state of consciousness at the time. This is suggested by the temporary suspension of her full reflective and critical faculties which made her, so strangely, more concerned about the possibility of the dog waking the village than about the fact that she was apparently witnessing an event from 1300 years ago. The cause of such an alteration in consciousness might have been related to exhaustion and cold and perhaps to the moment of apprehension, at the start of the experience, when she avoided the otherwise welcome short-cut near the end of her long and tiring walk.

That leaves the elaborate content of the experience. The first possibility to be considered here is that this was based upon forgotten knowledge acquired by a reading of Dr Wainwright's paper, or by a forgotten hearing of discussion about his findings or about the survey work upon which they had been based.

Miss Smith said she had previously heard of the Battle of Nechtanesmere, but not known who had fought there. She also said that she had heard of Dr Wainwright, but had not met him before the occurrence, although she did meet him after it. When I reminded her of the important fact that Dr Wainwright had published his paper just two years *before* her experience, and asked her bluntly if she had any recollection of having seen, or heard of, the paper beforehand, she said, "I had not seen it before I saw this. Someone gave it to me after, to read, but I merely told him I was one up on him!"

Regarding the vision being based on memory and not recognised as such by her, are there grounds to suspect the apparently correct location of the tip of the north-easterly finger of the mere? My own opinion is that it would have required a practised map-reader (which I found that Miss Smith certainly was not) to have transferred Dr Wainwright's mapped information so precisely and so correctly on to the landscape as viewed from the part of the road where she was.

Such doubts about a simple explanation in terms of an unrecognised memory lead on to the possibility of some form of paranormal hypothesis, possibly from the preoccupations of Dr Wainwright and his colleagues only three years earlier, and unconsciously stored in Miss Smith's mind.

No doubt he and his co-workers would have been very much preoccupied with details of the battle, and its nocturnal aftermath, and their thoughts would have been filled out by their expert knowledge both of the actual history of the battle and of the Picts and of what is known of their mode of dress.

However, certain features of the apparition appear to be unrelated to any features made explicit in Dr Wainwright's paper—e.g. (1) the extension so far east of the searching (presumably by the Picts) for their dead, (2) the details of clothing, and in particular, the curious detail of the headgear and (3) the redness of the torches.

Miss Smith had the impression that the figures wore "head-rings" for carrying things. She did not claim to have seen these used for the transport of bodies by Picts

Miss Smith's destination was Kirkden House on the edge of Letham, her home up to the time of her death in the late 1970s.   PHOTO: JOHN RUNDLE

working in pairs. Nevertheless it is surely possible, that the ancient Picts, like present-day Africans, were in the habit of carrying burdens on their heads and of wearing a hard ring for this purpose. That corpses might have been carried in this way would seem to be the sort of detail which might well be confirmed in the future as a result of increased knowledge about Pictish practices.

These additional features raise for consideration at least the possibility of a more general paranormal hypothesis, in terms of "retrocognition" or of some kind of collective knowledge and memory stores in what the psychiatrist C. G. Jung called the "collective unconscious," which, under certain circumstances, can be drawn upon. If so, it would be relevant to note that

Miss Smith was not the first person to experience an apparition about Nechtanesmere.

History reliably records that St Cuthbert, visiting Carlisle on the same Saturday afternoon as the battle, and viewing the Roman remains there, had a vision of the disaster which had befallen the Northumbrians.

He exclaimed, before witnesses, "Oh! Oh! Oh! I believe the war is ended, and the verdict has been given against our warriors."

History also records, but less reliably, that Bishop Wilfrid in Sussex while saying Mass (perhaps before light on the Sunday morning following the battle) had a vision of the soul of the slain Ecgfrith being carried off to Hell by two evil spirits. Is it possible that he had a telepathic vision of the aftermath of the battle and that the two "evil spirits" he saw were really two Picts (such as Miss Smith saw) carrying away, by the light of flaming torches, the body of Ecgfrith, and that they were interpreted by Wilfrid as evil spirits carrying him to Hell, partly because of the flames he saw and partly because he considered Ecgfrith deserved that fate? ◧

DID YOU HEAR ABOUT . . .

THE VANISHING HITCH-HIKER?

She probably never existed in the first place, claims **Gordon McCulloch**, who explains that it is only one of the many colourful, but legendary tales being told up and down the country today.

In the course of researching articles in folklore journals, I once came upon the tale of the suicide of Adam Clark, the English engineer who designed the Chain Bridge in Budapest in 1842. According to this story, Clark threw himself into the Danube during the opening ceremony after a passing message-boy remarked that the ornamental lions on his bridge ramparts had no tongues.

It seems that this story is still widely believed in Budapest, although it has absolutely no foundation in fact. The truth is that Clark returned to England and built many other bridges, while the missing lions' tongues were broken off long after the original construction.

The tale had the ring of familiarity to my ears for it brought to mind the story ("common knowledge" to Glasgow folk) of the architect of the Kelvingrove Art Gallery and Museum who is said to have taken his life when he discovered that his building had been built back to front.

In fact, two architects designed the building: J. W. Simpson and E. J. Milner Allan. Neither committed suicide nor was there any reason for them to do so, since the Gallery was built precisely as intended. The truth is that Kelvingrove Art Gallery was built to coincide with the Glasgow Exhibition of 1901. It was erected in conjunction with a number of temporary pavilions at what is now the rear of the building. Because of this it was provided with a rather more grand rear entrance than would normally be expected, a fact which became more noticeable after the pavilions had been removed.

So far, in my investigation of similar tales, I have unearthed 14 instances of Scottish architects and sculptors who are said to have committed suicide because of some fault in their work, and I suspect that this may be only the tip of a very substantial iceberg, for Scotland is littered with accounts of hara-kiri among public artists.

There is, for example, the story of the architect of Fort George, Inverness-shire. He, apparently, had been given instructions that the fort should not be visible from the seaward approach, presumably because of the risk of Jacobite attack. On completion of the work, he is said to have rowed out into the bay—and noticed that one small corner of a chimney could be seen. There and then he drew a revolver and blew out his brains.

Tales of suicidal sculptors also seem to be particularly popular in Glasgow. The plaid on the Sir Walter Scott statue in George Square is on the right (or "wrong") shoulder. Its sculptor, Baron Marochetti, is said to have killed himself when his error

was noticed. The same fate allegedly befell John Greenshields of Lesmahagow when it was discovered that a spur was missing from the left foot on his statue of the Duke of Wellington in Queen Street. In fact the missing spur was obviously broken off by vandals or souvenir-hunters in much more recent times. According to writer Jack House, John Greenshields died in his bed in 1835.

Stories of this kind also grow up around buildings that have aroused controversy, such as Marischal College in Aberdeen. For some, Marischal College was a trium-

Fort George in Inverness-shire. Folklore tells of the architect shooting himself when he discovered that part of a chimney could be observed from the sea thus breaching the terms of his commission. He had been told that the installation should be invisible from the sea.

PHOTO: SCOTTISH DEVELOPMENT DEPARTMENT

phant example of the elaborate perpendicular Gothic style. For others, however, it was a "monster-masterpiece" and "a wedding-cake in indigestible grey icing". This architect, too, is said to have taken his life because of such criticism.

So far as I have been able to ascertain, there is no truth in these, or in any other similar tales told and believed the length and breadth of Scotland.

So how do they arise, why do they spread so quickly and why do they "stick" so tenaciously? Since the Sixties, the attention of folklorists, in Scotland and in many other countries, has been increasingly attracted to these modern folktales, usually referred to as "contemporary legends" or "urban belief tales".

The localised legends mentioned above are just one aspect of a much broader range of modern folk tales; a range that includes an astonishing variety of story-types passed around by word of mouth. There are supernatural tales, grisly tales of unnatural death, tragi-comic tales of domestic calamity, comic tales of misadventure, and a host of others. What they have in common is that they are, for the most part, believed to be true accounts of real events, when in fact they have been told and retold in different versions in many countries, often over a considerable period. So in discussing "Scottish legends" we have to keep in mind that such tales are mostly Scottish *versions* of tales that are internationally told, just like many of the more familiar kinds of folklore—folksongs and ballads, fairytales, traditional beliefs, customs, proverbs, jokes and so on.

One of the best-known and most widely-travelled legends is "The Vanishing Hitch-hiker", which has been collected as far afield as Hawaii and Australia. It goes as follows: a driver picks up a young girl hitch-hiker, usually on a wild night, and agrees to take her to the address she gives. On arriving at her home he turns round to find that she has vanished into thin air. He knocks at the door and a woman answers it. He describes the girl and it transpires that she was the woman's daughter, and that she was killed in a road accident exactly ten years before at the spot where the driver picked her up.

One version, collected in Bridge of Allan, has an older man as the hitch-hiker. He and the driver discover a common interest in chess and on the road they discuss a chess problem but do not complete it. The hitch-hiker gets out of the car saying that he will leave the solution in a vase in his house so that the motorist can call some time and ask a member of the household to let him see it. He then disappears. Again the hitcher turns out to have died years before at the same spot, but a piece of paper with the chess solution is found in the vase.

Ghost stories in modern legend are, however, surprisingly rare, although there is scarcely a hospital in the country that does not have its "Grey Lady".

The Grey Lady at Hawkhead Mental Hospital in Paisley, for example, is said to be the ghost of a ward sister murdered by a patient many years ago. Again, according to the authors of a book on the Glasgow Subway, it has a Grey Lady, the ghost of a woman killed in 1921, who has been seen by maintenance staff on the nightshift.

Supernatural tales can also be topical. For instance, there was a widespread story in the Clydebank area concerning the sinking of the *HMS Ardent* during the Falklands War in 1982. A picture of the ship is said to have fallen off the wall of a pub near her birthplace, Yarrow's Shipyard, at precisely the moment she went down. Similar stories have been told since the time of the Battle of Jutland at least, and most likely a good deal longer.

The missing spur on the Duke of Wellington's statue in Glasgow's Queen Street is said to have been the cause of sculptor John Greenshields' suicide. The reality is that the spur was broken off by vandals and Mr Greenshields died in his bed.　　　　STAFF PHOTOGRAPHER

Perhaps the folklorist is best advised to take a strictly neutral attitude to these matters; to assume that "there are more things in heaven and earth . . ."

Modern supernatural tales are now relatively rare, but legends of grim and macabre events, usually ending in gory death, are very commonly encountered. Tales like "The Boyfriend's Death" seem to have begun life in the United States, but they are well known in Scotland, too, having been collected as early as the 1950s, and they are still circulating.

In one version a young couple are courting in their parked car somewhere on the Gleniffer Braes, near Paisley. On the radio they hear that a madman has escaped from the local asylum. Their car fails to start and

The statue of Sir Walter Scott in Glasgow's George Square. Baron Marochetti, the sculptor, is said to have killed himself when it was pointed out that the plaid had been placed over the wrong shoulder.

STAFF PHOTOGRAPHER

the boy goes to get help, making the girl promise not to open the car for any reason whatever. After a time, she begins to hear scratching noises on the car roof. These continue until dawn, with the girl too terrified to move. Eventually the police come and she is led away, after being told on no account to look back. Needless to

say, she does so, and sees that the scratching had been caused by the decapitated body of her boyfriend swinging by his heels from a tree.

The same tale, with the local details altered, turned up in Aberdeen in 1974 and a similar story concerns another young courting couple who hear on their car radio of the escape of a madman who has a hook in place of a hand. Shortly after, they hear scratching noises at the car doors and the terrified boy starts the car and roars off. When they arrive home they find a man's arm attached by a hook to the car door handle.

A number of tales of horrific death are told by steel and shipbuilding workers on Clydeside. At a Lanarkshire steelworks, for instance, I came across the story of the first-day apprentice who was put to work with his father. The boy was larking about and fell feet first into a ladle of molten metal. With only his head above the liquid steel, he screamed for help to his father. Realising that it was all up with his son, he ignored the screams and pushed him under with his foot.

Then, there's the popular tale of the riveter said to have been accidentally imprisoned inside the hull of the *Great Eastern*, the first of the double-bottom hulls. According to legend, the unfortunate victim was not discovered until decades later when the ship was broken up. On the bulkhead he had scrawled a message of farewell to his loved ones. It need hardly be said that legends of this kind have to be heard, rather than read, to appreciate the intensely dramatic charge that they carry.

However, not all legends share this almost Gothic engrossment with death and disaster. Some modern folktales concentrate instead on bizarre circumstances that have a calamitous outcome, but which nevertheless hold a comic appeal. One such is the celebrated legend of "Granny's Missing Corpse" (or "The Runaway Granny") in which a family on a touring holiday abroad are confronted with a problem when Granny dies suddenly. Not wishing to become involved with foreign officialdom, they decide to wrap her in a travelling rug, strap her to the roof-rack, and return home at once. En route, they stop at a restaurant for a meal and while they are dining, the car is stolen, Granny and all, never to be seen again.

Another very popular legend is the story of the housewife who is washing her pet poodle. Because she is in a hurry she decides to dry it in the microwave oven. (In some versions it is a baby instead of a poodle!) The poor creature is then said to have been cooked from the inside out, or alternatively to have exploded.

Cats and budgies, as well as dogs, frequently appear as the victims of modern legends. One concerns the body of a woman's dead cat. Not wishing to consign the corpse of the loved animal to the mercies of the rubbish collectors, she places it in a plastic bag to take it to the SSPCA, but the bag is stolen by a sneak-thief.

Budgies perish with alarming regularity in legendary accounts, stuck for eternity to their perches or silenced forever, the victims of superglue. My own favourite among budgie legends is the tale of the man who has just finished laying a fitted carpet, only to find that a single exasperating lump mars his work. He bashes it flat with a large hammer, and shortly after, notices that Joey is not in his cage!

It would be pleasant, out of respect for our friends in the Fourth Estate, to be able to state that modern legends are transmitted only by word of mouth. Alas, it is not so. Hoary old folktales appear and reappear in the Press with conspicuous regularity in the guise of reports of true occurrences. Sandy Hobbs, of the Social Studies Department at Paisley College, has been monitoring such "reports" for many years. An example from his substantial files is the story of "The Stolen Police Car" which concerns a man who leaves a party after a night of carousing and foolishly drives home. The police arrive at the house the following morning and demand to see his vehicle. Inside his garage stands a police car.

Modern legends, unlike the old fairy-tales, do not take place in an impossible stylised "wonderland" of castles and beautiful princesses. Instead, they are deeply rooted in the real life of our day-to-day world. They are told by young and old, men and women, bankers and dockers alike. They may be heard in pubs or at sewing bees; in a disco or on top of a bus; in a football crowd or around the fireside: in fact, just about any place where folk get together and blether.

Of course, I have been able to touch on only a handful of the many hundreds, perhaps thousands, of these modern folktales. Although there seems little doubt that many of them carry social morals within them, they are passed on mainly for entertainment, even if they are believed to be true.

With the more macabre legends, the entertainment comes from the vicarious thrill they provide. Tales such as the cancerous piece of liver that a housewife puts in her fridge, and which is later discovered feeding on a bottle of milk. Or the story of the couple who come home to find their Doberman dog choking. They rush him to the vet who operates immediately and extracts two human fingers from the animal's throat. In some versions the police are called and they discover a terrified and bloodstained burglar hiding in a wardrobe at the couple's home.

Many such tales have been on the go for a very long time indeed. Folklorist Shirley Marchalonis has discovered a tale in a 14th century mediaeval exemplum concerning a young woman who died after spiders had bored into her skull. The insects were said to have nested in her *beau soleil* hairstyle because she did not wash it. Many of us will recall the identical story being told about the young woman with the lacquered bee-hive hairdo in the 1960s.

The range of humorous legends is equally wide. There is the tale of the family who receive a package of powder from relatives abroad. They use it to make an omelette which tastes awful. Two weeks later comes a letter asking if Uncle Jim's ashes have arrived safely. Then there is the perennial tale of the circus elephant said to have crushed a bubble-car (or Mini, or Citröen 2CV, or Volkswagen Beetle) by sitting on it in mistake for a performing stool.

Perhaps I should conclude by mentioning some of the tales about our national game of football. In the aftermath of Celtic's 1967 European Cup triumph in Portugal, a number of legendary tales floated to the surface. I have been assured that one Celtic fan, hitch-hiking his way home, refused a lift to Castlemilk from Lisbon because he was making for Drumchapel. Then there was the supporter who'd imbibed too freely and was bundled by the exasperated Lisbon Police on to a Glasgow-bound plane along with hundreds of other fans. In some versions of this story he arrives at Glasgow Airport, having sobered up, only to remember that he'd travelled to Lisbon by car. An alternative version is that the unfortunate Scot was not in Lisbon for the match at all, but was on his honeymoon.

These stories might be believable were it not for the fact that similar tales are told in Manchester and Liverpool of their football teams.

Perhaps the football tale that stretches credulity beyond its limit is the one reported in an English newspaper shortly after Scotland's humiliating defeat by Peru in the 1978 World Cup. According to the writer, the only Peruvian llama in Glasgow Zoo was under round-the-clock guard.

It would be fascinating to know how many readers' memories have been jogged by reading these stories. Certainly I would be most interested to hear new folktales, or different versions of the same ones. I guarantee to swallow them with the heartiest appetite . . . and perhaps just a pinch of salt. ⏻

INVESTIGATIONS

OBAN'S OTHER FOLLY

Robin Shaw

Not many places are lucky, or unlucky enough to possess a folly. Oban has two and both occupy very prominent positions in the town.

McCaig's Tower, as it is correctly styled, is the better-known. The other structure is not nearly so familiar.

Stand in busy Argyll Square, raise your eyes above the nose-to-tail tourist throng and you will see the town's Hydro. Jutting above the lip of an old sea-cliff, a quarter of a mile from the harbour, is a group of quaint ruins which, a century ago, were destined to be Oban's answer to Dunblane, Rothesay or Pitlochry. The Hydropathic Establishment and Sanitorium was a grandiose project made for the age of speculation and enterprise.

The *Oban Times* of 28th May 1881 editorialised with local pride (and real justification) that "the site is perhaps the best that could possibly be obtained in the Kingdom". With a confidence that later proved to be sadly misplaced, the paper suggested that the project should provide "a productive outlet to the capital of shareholders".

Certainly the *Oban Times* seemed right to have confidence. This was truly an age of expansion, for the west coast in general and Oban in particular. The recently opened railway was bringing the gentry and the well-to-do in ever increasing numbers. Had not Queen Victoria herself declared Oban to be "one of the finest spots we have seen"? Private yachts thronged the bay, much as they do now in Cannes or Nice, and the formation of the Royal Highland Yacht Club was imminent. The modern age was dawning—Oban played host to its first Electric Exhibition.

Naturally enthusiasm ran high when a large group of shareholders in the new Oban Hills Hydropathic and Sanatorium Company gathered in the Company offices in Bath Street, Glasgow, on Thursday, 17th May 1881 to view and discuss the plans.

This was not the first meeting of the Company. To the disappointment of the architect, Mr J. Ford Mackenzie of Glasgow, and several others, an earlier meeting of December 1880 had become concerned at the proposed expenditure of £75,000 and had sent the plans back for revision.

Now a reduced plan of expenditure had been produced and the architectural and perspective drawings were unveiled to an eager audience. A remarkable feat of surgery had been performed and the cost was to be only £32,000.

The recently completed Pitlochry Hydropathic had cost upwards of £100,000. On that building, the Chairman, Dr Robert Orr assured the meeting, £40,000 to £50,000 had been wasted in extravagances. This was not to happen at Oban. Tenders had been received well within the proposed £32,000. However, this was to be no cut-price establishment. Oban's position as one

This is how the Oban Hydropathic Hotel was planned to look. Had it been completed it would almost certainly still be flourishing today, occupying as it does a prime site above the bay.

of the most fashionable resorts in the country demanded excellence and style.

The proposed hotel was to have 137 bedrooms for guests and adequate provision for their servants. Specially designed Turkish baths were planned as was a large seawater plunge-bath. Since the Hydropathic would be 100 feet above sea level, strong and reliable pumps were required. When you consider the lack of a sewage treatment scheme and the large number of craft in the bay, I hope that efficient filters were to be used.

A private gasworks was designed to produce the necessary light and heat and there were also to be stables, a laundry, workshops and an imposing gate lodge. The design called for a main building that would be airy and spacious with lofty corridors and modern stained-glass everywhere. A recreation and concert hall, a winter garden and fernery, and a golf course were to complete the amenities.

One unusual feature was the wide use of hydraulic lifts connecting every floor. There were even plans to connect the hotel to the town below by a lift in which guests would arrive.

Even making allowances for the difference in the value of money today—the manager of the hotel was to receive an annual salary of £200—£32,000 seems a meagre amount for such grandiose plans.

A note of caution was sounded at the meeting by Mr Hunter of Denny. Not unreasonably he said, "I know from my own experience that estimates are sometimes considerably below actual prices." He received little sympathy. The late 19th century was not an era of commercial caution.

Mr Lawrence, the Town Clerk of Oban,

had no such doubts. "If I had this grand-looking view of the building hung in my business room at Oban, I am sure I could place several shares among my Oban clients and friends. Oban hotels are doing a very considerable stroke of business and I am really sure that the Sanitorium would be doing a very large business by April. No one," he concluded, "need be afraid of realising a good profit."

Dr Orr, the Chairman, was the very model of confidence. Tenders had been received at the prices estimated and the situation was eased by the low cost of wages and materials. This hydropathic establishment, while being the finest, would also be the cheapest to build in England or Scotland. With its Scottish baronial style, it would give Oban a "skyline broken by towers and turrets and other quaint looking features."

Everything was to be built of the local bluish stone found on site. Moreover, if the meeting accepted the tenders proposed by Robert McAlpine and Company of Hamilton for the masonry and brickwork, and by J. McCormack and Company of Glasgow for the carpentry, the establishment would be in operation by the summer of 1882.

There were a few more mutterings from Mr Hunter, but the fact that both McAlpine and McCormack were happy to receive a large part of their contract sums in the form of shares seemed to allay any doubts.

The meeting passed the contracts and Dr Orr wound up the proceedings, telling the shareholders that success was assured by "the worldwide fame that Oban has attained as a watering place, the immense number of people who frequent it, and the revolution this new railway has effected." In a closing sentence he encapsulated the 19th century attitude to business, an attitude that now seems more than a century removed from us. "There is nothing reasonable," the Chairman said, "that a determined man or company cannot attain if they set about it."

By the 4th June, operations had commenced. The site had formerly been a planted garden and palms were uprooted to make room for the foundations. An entrance drive was to be blasted out of the rock along the top of the cliff from Ardconnel Road. Here the first snag was encountered as the rock was found to be much harder than supposed. Nevertheless, by 27 August the carriageway was almost complete and the concrete foundations were laid.

A steam engine was in position at the top of the cliff and a line of rails was laid down the precipitous slope into the town to a point near the goods station. Up this line, building materials were drawn in a series of wagons using a large steam-driven windlass.

By 17 December, the *Oban Times* was reporting that the Hydropathic was now a conspicuous landmark in the town. The builders had reached the third storey. Already, despite the pace of building, it was becoming apparent that optimism had ruled the heads of the planners. The local stone, the use of which was meant to provide great savings, was found to be useless since it had copper in it and proved to be too friable. Sandstone blocks had to be imported as a substitute. Much more blasting than was planned for had been necessary.

Like all large building enterprises, the Hydropathic had its share of accidents, though luckily none of them was fatal. Scaffolding collapsed in February 1882, and three men fell 30 feet from the north-east corner, escaping wth minor injuries. Two months later, a Dundee mason, John McLauchlan, was knocked from the wall, 40 feet up, by the box of a crane. He sustained several broken bones and was slow to recover.

By the spring of 1882 the operation had run into serious trouble. Much of the subscribed capital had been absorbed by the costly blasting and importation of stone.

Building operations ceased, men were paid off and the half-finished structure was exciting adverse comments locally. The original shareholders could or would go no further and were reduced to selling off their holdings. An English company bought them up and after a short gap the work was resumed.

Oban and the *Oban Times* breathed again. "The roof is on a portion of the building, while the grounds are being put into shape," the paper reported on 22nd June 1882. "It is to be hoped," the editor declared, "that the building operations at this monster erection of stone and concrete will now go forward on a more prosperous path than hitherto."

Alas, it was not to be. Despite the good intentions of the new company and the fact that the building had reached an advanced stage, the enterprise foundered. The main structure had been so close to completion that a special visit had been made by Mr Rutherford, the photographic artist, to take views of it.

The *Oban Times*, which had heralded the new venture with confidence and enthusiasm, now, a year and a half later on 2nd December 1882, wrote its epitaph:

Oban Hydro shortly before all work ceased. Compare the incomplete shell with the artist's impression on page 46 to see how closely the reality would have filled the dream.

The Oban Hydro in miniature. This fine villa, built in 1903, stands at the end of the drive where a lodge was proposed. The stonework came from the ruins of the unfinished hotel and cost £10. The house itself was erected for £300.

PHOTO: JOHN RUNDLE

D

The ruined Hydro today from the same angle as the other illustrations. Much of the stone was removed by local builders and used to construct houses in the town.   PHOTO: JAMES MCEWAN

"The operations have ceased at the Hydropathic. The contractor has removed all his moveable plant and the window openings on the different floors have been boarded up. The slater carted away all the slates he had on the ground and a portion of the building will doubtless be left without a covering, though the sarking is on the roof timbers. The whole building is a monument to the folly of commencing to build before counting the cost, and anything but an ornament in its present condition in Oban."

Several attempts to raise capital to complete the project came to nothing. One in 1896 included directors of the Madras Railway Company and Longs Hotel, Bond Street, London. It invited subscriptions of a total of £250,000, but the necessary funds were not forthcoming.

Over the years the property has passed through many hands including Dorrans of Perth, the builders, and Dr Green who achieved notoriety through his ownership of Raasay.

And so the age of hydropathics, Turkish baths and seawater plunge-pools passed Oban by.

Much of the stone went to other buildings on the hill. Mr William Hunter, the Oban councillor, recalls blasting in the Thirties and several large blocks of stone rolling dangerously into the town. Several fine villas now have walls of Hydropathic sandstone.

The ruins that are left have attained the respectability and romance of age and are now seen more as an asset than an eyesore.

Because of a freak in translation, a German travel guide speaks tantalisingly of the hydro-electric scheme on the hill in Oban, but to most locals and visitors, the ruined Hydropathic is Oban's second folly.

THE TRAGEDY OF BARRIE AND BAIRD

W. D. BERNARD

Little more than 50 years have passed since Hugh Barrie and Thomas Baird lost their lives under tragic circumstances while climbing in the Cairngorms. This was an event which in those days caused something of a sensation, and aroused deep and widespread sympathy throughout the country. Theirs was an epic struggle for survival against overwhelming odds—the elements at their wildest on one of the highest and most exposed parts of the Cairngorm massif. It was a great battle, bravely fought, and sadly lost.

Apart from keepers, shepherds, and those whose occupation and way of life necessitated them frequenting the hills, comparatively few people indulged in hill-walking during the earlier years of the century. Since the late Fifties, however, this form of outdoor activity has become widely recognised as a sport in its own right and countless people now make for the hills at all seasons of the year.

Inevitably, accidents occur, many because of the fact that some people go improperly clad, with no idea of prevailing conditions or how to act in an emergency. It is not at all surprising, therefore, that the hills, and in particular the Cairngorms, have taken a heavy toll of human life.

While these tragedies are in every way as harrowing as that of Barrie and Baird, they have become so commonplace, as to evoke little notice from the public in general. Occurring when it did, the Barrie and Baird tragedy made a profound impact on public imagination, and even tended to become tinged with a slight element of romance.

Hugh Barrie and Thomas Baird, both graduates of Glasgow University, arrived in Aviemore on Wednesday 28th December 1927, their intention being to spend a few days climbing in the Cairngorms. A brief visit on an earlier occasion had whetted their appetite to spend a longer period in the midst of such grand surroundings and their ambition seemed about to be realised. In Aviemore they made a number of purchases, then set about finding cheap and suitable accommodation.

Maggie Gruer, that grand old lady of Inverey near Braemar, provided both food and shelter for countless walkers and climbers in the Cairngorms, but unfortunately, she had no counterpart in the Aviemore district. Luck was with the two young men on this occasion, however, for at Whitewell, a small croft a few miles south-east of Aviemore, occupied by a Mr and Mrs McKenzie, they were given accommodation in which to spend the night.

Mrs McKenzie immediately took to the two young men, and went out of her way to help them, lighting a fire to warm their room, and providing a good meal. That evening Barrie and Baird outlined their plans to their hosts: setting out early in the morning, they intended to make for the Corrour Bothy in the Lairig Ghru, and, using it as a base, do a number of climbs. They meant to return in a few days by way of Glen Einich.

The McKenzies were most unhappy at the thought of two young men, with comparatively little experience of the mountains, undertaking such a programme in midwinter, particularly as the weather was unsettled at the time and seemed likely to remain so for some days. They did their utmost to dissuade them from setting out, but to no avail. On the morning of 29th December, Barrie and Baird left the house on the journey which was destined to end in tragedy.

The traverse of the Lairig Ghru is the finest and most exciting hillwalking expedition in Scotland. As seen from near Coylumbridge, the main point of access to the Cairngorms from Speyside, it appears as a great V-shaped defile running due south between Ben Macdhui on the left and Braeriach standing opposite and it provides the shortest and most direct link between Coylum and Braemar, a total distance of 22 miles. From Coylumbridge the route to the Lairig leads for a time through part of the Rothiemurchus Forest, before commencing the steep climb to reach the mouth of the Pass. At this point the forest is left behind for the shadow of the cliff-crowned summit, familiarly known as the Lurcher's Crag.

The head of the Lairig is reached at an altitude of 2733 ft. and the going becomes very difficult, as a number of boulder-fields have to be crossed. Before descending into the Aberdeenshire sector, three little pools are passed. These, all connected by subterranean channels, are the Pools of Dee, one of the sources of the River Dee.

The scene which now unfolds is breathtaking in its grandeur and wildness. On the right, Braeriach comes into view, forming, with Sgor an Lochain Uaine and Cairn Toul, a vast amphitheatre, An Garbh Choire, rarely surpassed for ruggedness and majesty. The loneliness and utter desolation of the place serves only to enhance the sheer magnificence of the surroundings. Down this deep recess comes the little burn from the Wells of Dee high up on Braeriach to join the one trickling ice-cold and clear from the Pools.

Beyond Cairn Toul, one of the most shapely of all the Cairngorm summits, stands the Devil's Point, a great bluff, and the dominating feature of the mountain landscape at the south end of the pass. Rising to 3303 ft. it lies almost directly opposite the glen which leads to Derry Lodge. Its unusual formation of great slabs of rock, which have been aptly described as "titanic masonry," and its apparent inaccessibility, gives it a most forbidding aspect.

At the base is the Corrour Bothy, the only shelter between Rothiemurchus and the Linn of Dee. Consisting of one room, it was built in 1877 to house a deer-watcher, and continued to be used for this purpose until 1914. After the war it became a haven for walkers and climbers, for which it is ideally suited and sited.

It was into this great wilderness of boulder and mountain that Barrie and Baird walked soon after leaving Whitewell. Despite a fair amount of snow lying around in the Lairig, they made good progress, arriving at Corrour without mishap well before darkness closed in. After a comfortable night they set out early next morning to climb the Devil's Point, using the path which starts uphill immediately behind the bothy leading to the ridge which gives easy access to the summit.

In the late afternoon they returned to the bothy, and after eating they settled down to plan a more extended outing for the following day. These plans were made in vain for, during the night, there was a dramatic change in the weather, and they were soon experiencing the full force of a winter storm in the very heart of the Cairngorms.

These mountains are very exposed to the cold, snow-bearing winds which blow from the north and east and, in consequence, receive abnormally heavy falls of

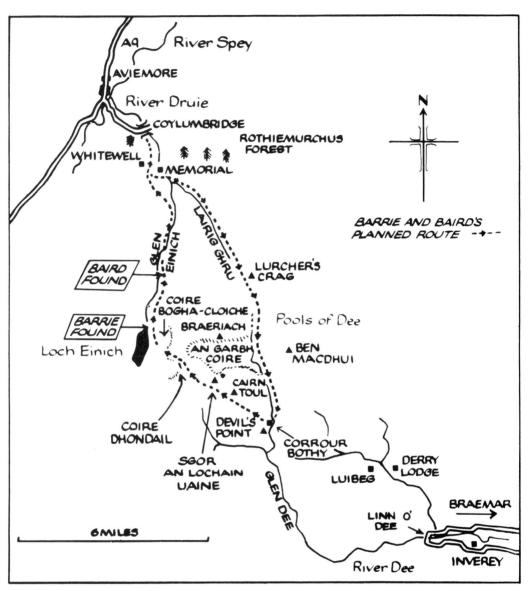

Map showing the route taken by the two climbers.

snow. In winter, storms of great severity can rage, conditions on the higher ground becoming sub-arctic with temperatures as low as minus 20° F. Hurricane-force winds can blow up suddenly, making it quite impossible to stand upright, and blinding blizzards make it not only difficult to breathe, but virtually impossible to see any distance ahead.

The severe blizzard continued to rage with unabated fury throughout the following day, while the temperature dropped steadily. By nightfall a severe frost set in, and conditions became truly arctic. Their

[53]

boots froze, and Barrie and Baird had to sit on them for a prolonged period until they thawed out sufficiently to be worn. The Primus—a most vital piece of equipment for cooking and heating—failed to function. Added to this, their food supply was running dangerously low, and there were absolutely no means of replenishing their stock. In short, the situation was becoming desperate. They must have realised that, with conditions steadily deteriorating, their one chance of survival depended entirely on their being able to leave the bothy at daybreak, no matter the prevailing weather conditions.

It is easy to imagine the thoughts which tormented them during the long, tedious day of solitary confinement at the bothy. Face to face with the greatest crisis of their lives, their confidence in their own ability to control their destiny must have rapidly melted away as they realised the frailty of man when pitted against the remorseless fury of Nature in her wildest mood. How bitterly now they must have regretted their failure to accept the sound advice of the McKenzies before setting out from Whitewell.

On Sunday, New Year's Day, they awoke to a bright, sunny morning, with the surrounding tops standing out clearly against an azure blue sky. The portents were not good, however: a red sky toward the east, and great storm clouds massing ominously on the horizon, heralded another blizzard. Perhaps these signs passed unnoticed for by eight o'clock they were on their way.

The route they planned to follow was to make the ascent to the ridge behind Corrour Bothy, and, crossing over Cairn Toul, strike the summit plateau of Braeriach, thence making the descent into Glen Einich. The walk from the Devil's Point to Braeriach has been described as the finest high-level traverse in the UK. A distance of three and a half miles, it can be accomplished under reasonable conditions in just under two hours.

About ten o'clock the storm broke. The two climbers would have reached the higher ground about this time, and would, therefore, be completely exposed to the merciless hurricane-force winds and blinding snow. The movements of the two men up to this point were briefly recorded by Baird in his diary, though the last entries were scarcely legible, no doubt due to numbed fingers being unable to control the pencil.

From about the time of their arrival on Braeriach, we can only surmise what happened. They certainly must have been reduced to crawling, and, when descending Coire Bogha-cloiche, immediately to the north of Coire Dhondail, they completely lost contact with one another, due to darkness, the storm, or even the possibility of a glissade. Had they been able to keep together, they might well have reached the safety of the Upper Bothy, near the head of Glen Einich.

I mentioned that the movements of the two men since their departure from Corrour could only be surmised, but there were certain clues which cast light upon their progress from the bothy onwards. It would have been natural for them to descend from the summit of Braeriach into Coire Dhondail rather than into Coire Bogha-cloiche, which is much more precipitous. The fact that their rucksacks were found in Coire Bogha-cloiche, at about 3000 ft. suggests they came down by the more hazardous route.

Baird reached the foot of Braeriach near the bothy before he stumbled in a snow wreath, bruised, battered, and completely exhausted, never to rise again. He was in a most pitiable condition, the skin of his left hand completely worn off, several fingers badly lacerated, his right knee injured. His breeches were badly torn at the knees, suggesting he had been forced to crawl a considerable distance. By cruel coincidence, the storm seemed to play itself out about the very time Baird fell, and a great calm fell over the glen.

Baird was found next day by two men out for a leisurely walk up Glen Einich. Alastair Cram and John McConnachie could scarcely believe their eyes when they saw a man lying prostrate by the side of the road, apparently sleeping. They soon realised the true situation, and carried him the short distance to the bothy. As they crossed the threshold, Baird's lips moved, and he expired almost immediately.

Leaving McConnachie at the bothy, Cram made his way down the glen as quickly as conditions would allow. Reaching Coylumbridge, he alerted Dr Balfour of Aviemore by phone. The doctor set off immediately by car and picked up Cram at Coylum.

The snow was so deep in the glen they were forced to turn back. Not to be beaten, however, they set out once more, using a horse and sleigh, a form of transport much more suited to the state of the track, and reached the bothy without difficulty. In the evening, under cover of darkness, they brought Baird's body down the glen to Aviemore.

The news of Baird's untimely death was widely reported in the Press. The main talking point now concerned the whereabouts of Hugh Barrie. Was he still alive, or had he perished in the same way as his friend? These were questions which, alas, were to remain unanswered for the time being.

The measure of public concern for Barrie's safety was reflected in the large number of people drawn from all walks of life who gathered in Glen Einich the day after the discovery of Baird, in order to search for the missing climber, a great effort which proved fruitless. A subsequent attempt to find him also failed, and it was decided to abandon any further search until weather conditions improved.

While the 60-strong party searched in Glen Einich, a smaller group was operating from the other end of the Lairig. Believing that Barrie might have decided to ride out the storm by remaining at Corrour Bothy, a party of six men including a few police, and led by Alex Grant of Luibeg, set out for Corrour.

Conditions were appalling. Walking in snow which was knee-deep, in a raging blizzard with visibility reduced to a few yards, their rate of progress was about one mile per hour. They struggled on, however, in ever worsening conditions to within a quarter mile of the bothy, until turned back by the police, who would permit no further risks to be taken. Personally, I very much doubt if the party was aware of the close proximity of the bothy when the decision was reached to proceed homewards.

On 14th January a second attempt was made to reach the bothy, this time successfully. When they looked inside, the bothy was empty. The only clue which pointed to it having been occupied recently were the footprints of the two men, frozen hard in the snow and leading to the ridge behind the building.

It was now clear that Barrie must be dead. No human being could possibly have survived so long in such freezing conditions amid these snowy wastes.

Nothing more could be done in the meantime: it was a case of waiting until the deep layer of winter snow melted and, just as the dusk fades into darkness, so the Barrie mystery receded into that

The Corrour Bothy with the Devil's Point behind. It was this former deer-watcher's dwelling that Barrie and Baird spent their last night.   PHOTO: B. H. HUMBLE

shadowy realm of things long forgotten.

Time went on but failed to produce any clue which might provide a solution to the mystery. Then, on 24th March, while walking in Coire Bogha-cloiche, John McKenzie, head stalker on the Rothiemur-chus Estate, and a son of Mr and Mrs McKenzie of Whitewell, found the rucksacks of the two men lying about 300 ft. apart.

In their descent from the summit of Braeriach, in a near exhausted condition, each of them had discarded his rucksack in an effort to lighten his load. This chance discovery pointed to the fact that Barrie was probably somewhere between the corrie and the foot of the mountain.

Next day, having been alerted by John McKenzie, a search party of six men from Nethybridge, and five from Aviemore, made for Glen Einich. Spreading out into an extended line, the party started up the mountain. While it was a mild day, and most of the snow had cleared, a fairly dense mist shrouded the familiar landmarks. Mr S. Slessor, Keeper at Drumintoul, had his Labrador retriever with him and it was the behaviour of the dog on reaching a certain point that led to the discovery of Barrie, lying in the peat-hag where he had fallen.

The body was in a wonderful state of preservation, despite the fact that it had lain there undisturbed for almost three months. Barrie was lying on his back, apparently sleeping, but, alas, it was the long sleep from which there is no awakening.

After keeping the world waiting, the mountain had at last yielded its secret, and revealed the mystery of the lost climber. Barrie's remains were brought down the glen to Whitewell that afternoon.

Barrie had already been presumed dead, and the legal process of settling his affairs had started. Among his belongings was a page of writing paper with a poem in the deceased's handwriting. It would have been obvious at once to anyone with a love of poetry, that this poem was a minor literary masterpiece.

With its remarkable imagery, and rare beauty of language, it expresses Barrie's wishes regarding his last resting-place and might well be described as his "last will and testament".

It is with these lines that the element of romance enters the story:

When I am dead
And this strange spark of life that in me lies
Is fled to join the great white core of life
That surely flames beyond eternities,
And all I ever thought of as myself
Is mouldering to dust and cold dead ash,
This pride of nerve and muscle—merest
dross,
This joy of brain and eye and touch but trash,
Bury me not, I pray thee,
In the dark earth where comes not any ray
Of light or warmth or aught that made life
dear,
But take my whitened bones, far, far away
Out of the hum and turmoil of the town.
Find me a windswept boulder for a bier
And on it lay me down,
Where far beneath drops sheer the rocky ridge
Down to the gloomy valley, and the streams
Fall foaming white against black beetling
rocks,
Where the sun's kindly radiance seldom
gleams;
Where some tall peak, defiant, steadfast,
mocks
The passing gods; and all the ways of men
forgotten.
So may I know
Even in that death that comes to everything
The silent swish of hurrying snow,
The lash of rain; the savage bellowing
Of stags; the bitter-keen knife-edge embrace
Of the rushing wind: and still the tremulous
dawn
Will touch the eyeless sockets of my face,
And I shall see the sunset and anon
Shall know the velvet kindness of the night,
And see the stars.

Sheriff J. P. Grant, Laird of Rothiemurchus, like countless others, had followed the gradual unfolding of the poignant drama, and had no doubt been given an opportunity to read the poem.

Deeply moved he made a touching

gesture by gifting a small piece of ground on a strip of moorland near Whitewell, where, it is believed, Celtic burials took place.

Barrie's funeral was on the afternoon of 27th March, only two days after the discovery of his body. It was a lovely spring day, when, about 3.30 p.m. the cortège moved out from Whitewell led by Mr McKenzie. The coffin, draped in the colours of the Glasgow University Officers' Training Corps and covered with wreaths of tulips, daffodils, carnations and evergreens, was carried the 200 yards to the place of interment by members of the Corps. The brief service was conducted by the Rev. S. Thomson of Newtonmore, Rev. J. Andrew, Baillieston Church, Glasgow, (of which Barrie was a member), and Rev. J. A. C. Murray, Park Parish Church, Glasgow. It was simple and deeply moving. By a strange coincidence, a brilliant rainbow hung in the eastern sky as the procession left Whitewell.

As the coffin was slowly lowered into its last resting place, the rainbow gradually melted away. Barrie's rucksack, clothing, and groundsheet, which he used on all his climbing expeditions, were dropped down into the grave.

The Rev. Mr Andrew took the committal, concluding most appropriately with the famous lines from R. L. Stevenson—

Under the wide and starry sky
Dig the grave and let me lie
Glad did I live and gladly die,
And I laid me down with a will.

This be the verse you grave for me:
"Here he lies where he longed to be:
Home is the sailor, home from sea,
And the hunter home from the hill."

A most poignant moment followed as Piper Simpson played the beautiful air "The Flowers o' the Forest" and, as the plaintive notes drifted away into silence, a deep hush descended upon the whole assembly, broken only by the eerie howl of a dog in the distance.

After the burial a large cairn was built over the grave, with a huge boulder of pink granite, roughly hewn, lying squarely on top. The inscription reads—

> In proud and affectionate memory
> of Hugh Alexander Barrie M. A.
> (Interred here)
> and Thomas Baird M. A.
> (Interred at Baldernock)
> who lost their lives on 2nd January
> 1928,
> while climbing these hills.
> "Find me a windswept boulder for a
> bier."

Thomas Baird was buried at Baldernock in Stirlingshire where, for many years, his father was the dominie and a much-loved member of the community. Some 300 mourners followed the cortège the mile from the school to the cemetery to pay their last respects.

The tragedy of Barrie and Baird demands our sympathy, but also commands great admiration. It is hard to comprehend the awful ordeal they endured. They certainly passed through the "Refiner's fire," and, in so doing, displayed the admirable qualities of courage, love of adventure, endurance and perseverance.

While engaged in filming Scottish rivers, I have walked extensively in the Cairngorms, and have experienced the irresistible spell of these great mountains. When holidaying each year in Speyside, I always feel drawn back to that hallowed spot on the moor near Whitewell, to pay my silent tribute to two kindred spirits.

I hope that the retelling of this tale will serve to keep the memory of two valiant hearts evergreen.

THE ACHALLADER LETTERS

Archie McKerracher recalls a climbing tragedy and the subsequent mysterious events which have never been satisfactorily explained.

On the morning of Sunday, 22nd March 1925, three young men set out from the Inveroran Hotel near Bridge of Orchy to climb nearby Ben Achallader, 3404 ft. Their outing was to end in tragedy, but out of this came an extraordinary chain of events which, some might say, would seem to confirm the existence of a spirit world.

Archibald MacLay Thomson, Douglas Ewen, and 30-year-old Alexander Lawson Henderson left the hotel at 5.30 a.m. They were well equipped and carried ice-axes although none had experience of the mountains in winter. Thomson was making the ascent as one of the six climbs necessary to qualify for admission to the Scottish Mountaineering Club. Alexander Henderson was the most proficient, having climbed in Europe during leave from his work with the Inland Revenue at Paisley where he had been transferred from his native Cupar.

The three went by the north shore of Loch Tulla to the ford on the Water of Tulla near Achallader Farm. They arrived at the railway line at 7.30 a.m. beside the cairn to a walker killed by a train, and stopped to survey the climb ahead. The day was clear, but extremely frosty, and they had been warned that the top slopes would be icy. They made their first mistake by deciding to ascend the mountain by a wide snow-gully which, to their inexperienced eyes, appeared to offer the easiest route to the summit.

They set off on a more or less direct line to the top, but the going turned out to be much harder than they expected, and by 9.30, when they stopped for breakfast, they were at only 2000 feet. Henderson was feeling the cold badly and could not sit still. He wandered around restlessly. At 10.30 he set off ten minutes ahead of his companions who kept him in sight until 11.15, when he bore over to the left, presumably to find an easier line, and they lost sight of him behind some rocks.

Thomson and Ewen encountered severe problems on the frozen snow in the gully, and higher up they were forced on to iced rocks. These were so hazardous that they agreed it would be impossible to descend by this route. They eventually struggled up to the summit cairn at 1.25 p.m. and were puzzled to find no trace of their friend. They wandered around for two hours, shouting his name and operating a hand siren, before Thomson lowered himself on a rope over the cornice of ice and snow to the ridge below. This was where Henderson should have been, but again there was no sign of him.

Thomson and Ewen then made for the col between Ben Achallader and Meall Buidhe to search the plateau for footprints. They found none and returned, baffled, to the cairn at 6 p.m. Ten minutes later, they set off again, and with great difficulty climbed to the summit of Meall Buidhe. They looked in all directions, but with darkness falling, they abandoned their search and stumbled downhill. They reached Achallader farm at 8.40 and were fed and rested by the farmer and his wife,

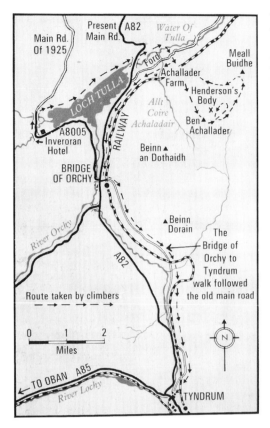

Map labels:
Main Rd. Of 1925
Present Main Rd.
A82
Water Of Tulla
Meall Buidhe
Ford
Achallader Farm
Henderson's Body ×
Allt Coire Achaladair
Ben Achallader
LOCH TULLA
RAILWAY
A8005
Inveroran Hotel
Beinn an Dothaidh
BRIDGE OF ORCHY
River Orchy
A82
Beinn Dorain
The Bridge of Orchy to Tyndrum walk followed the old main road
Route taken by climbers
- - → - → - →
0 1 2
Miles
N
TO OBAN A85
River Lochy
A85
TYNDRUM

Mr and Mrs Duncan Smith. The Smiths tried to persuade them to stay the night, but, convinced that by now Henderson had crossed over the hills to Tyndrum, Thomson and Ewen left Achallader at 10.35 p.m. to walk the 16 miles to the Royal Hotel. They arrived there in a state of collapse, at 3.45 on Monday morning, having covered 44 miles in 22½ hours.

The hotel proprietor, Robert Stewart, immediately raised the alarm. A full-scale search was organised by mid-morning, but, because of a mislaid telegram, it was Wednesday before teams of experienced climbers from the Scottish Mountaineering Club arrived from Glasgow and Edinburgh. A 15-mile radius around Ben Achallader

was soon thoroughly searched, although the work was hampered by snow and rain.

On Thursday 26th March, a most peculiar letter, postmarked Peterhead, but undated, arrived at the Royal Hotel. The envelope was addressed to a Mr Garret and it was decided it was for Mr Garrick, leader of one of the search parties. Garrick was a lecturer at the Royal Technical College, Glasgow, and an experienced mountaineer. The letter read:

"Dear Sir, This is going to be a difficult letter to write, and, beyond making use of the information it may give, I would ask you to be so good as to keep it to yourself as far as possible. A friend and myself have, within the last three months, received startling proof of the accuracy of the information regarding unknown people, which we have received from a supernatural agency—I cannot go into details of these now—it would serve no purpose.

"Yesterday (Tuesday 24th) it occurred to us that we might be able to get useful information as to the whereabouts of the lost Mr Henderson, and at 12 noon we approached the usual source of our information, and requested that a 'scout' be sent out to get any information possible. In the evening (about 6.30 p.m.) we asked for news, and the undernoted is verbatim: *The answer is slow in coming but our messenger now reports that it is raining, and one, I think his name is Cameron, is heading towards the col, where the man is lying. The snow is deep here, perhaps 20 feet, and it may be that Cameron is not sure of his feet and we cannot influence him sufficiently; it may be I say three, some say six, weeks ere he be found. Jim says he is warm yet . . .*

"(Later) Where may he be found? Can no directions be given?"

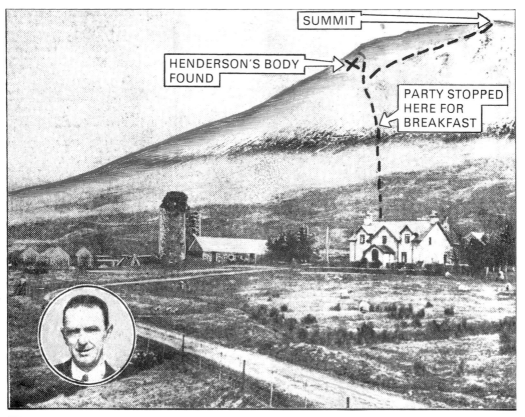

The layout from Achallader Farm with (inset) Duncan Smith.

"Such information as I have is scant, but the news is that he is warm, and we are not led to think he is asleep. What do you say of Death—there is no Death . . . (interruption) Where is he? *He has not yet passed, but his needs are worldly. It is a col. Ask one, I think his name is Cameron, where he was at 4 of the clock today. They are still searching, and we are trying to help.*

"Now, we do not know a single member of the search party, but should there be amongst them one of the name of Cameron, that would be one point correct, indicating an intelligence of some kind behind our information. I would say that in all probability the whole of the information as to location of the spot for which you are searching is correct, and that the information should not be treated lightly. Neither my friend nor myself are spiritualists, but interested in investigating phenomena we do not pretend to understand. In view of the nature of the information, we feel conscience bound to pass it on—it can do no harm and may be useful."

The letter was signed, "ANXIOUS TO HELP" and it aroused great curiosity, particularly when it was found that a Mr Cameron had indeed been on the col at 4 p.m. on the Tuesday, and that it had also been raining that day.

However, the letter was put aside as

preparations were made for a major search at the weekend. The weather had improved considerably, and on Sunday, 29th March, a plane was able to fly from Renfrew Aerodrome. It circled low over the hill where as many as 70 climbers could be seen crossing and recrossing the mountain. The glens below were scoured by slate workers from Ballachulish, shepherds, stalkers and police, but all to no avail. The searchers returned, completely baffled as to the whereabouts of Alexander Henderson.

On the following Saturday, a second letter arrived, postmarked 2nd April, Peterhead, and addressed this time to Robert Stewart of the Royal Hotel. This enclosed two sketches, and the writer stated that neither he nor his friend was acquainted with the locality so they could not say which way they should be read.

> "They are reputed to have been drawn for us by the 'scout' sent to the spot and the following is his information: *Leave Loch Tulla and go along the road until you come to Ford which lies between the castle and the Big House, and go up the corrie. You go east, and climb the corrie on your right hand.* Asked if nothing could be done, we were told that there would be no hope until a thaw for recovery of the body. My friend and myself would give our names but in view of the publicity, we prefer not to do so."

It was signed, "STILL ANXIOUS TO HELP".

Another letter, undated, arrived almost immediately, clarifying the reference as being the ford over the Water of Tulla. (The Big House was the local name for Achallader Farm.) The climbers were directed to:

> "*Follow the valley—some say corrie—to*

its source and at an altitude of 3060 feet they will get as close as I can tell you at present. We asked for a sketch of the place but our 'scout' was with the searcher called MaKlairen. You will know if one of that name is out."

One of the mountain rescue leaders was indeed a Captain MacLaren from Connel Ferry.

Then a fourth letter arrived, postmarked 3rd April, and giving its time of writing as 9 p.m.

> "There is so little to report. We have found a definite aid to the climbers. It is in the shape of a tin box. It is still visible. Has our letter to Garret been opened? *Yes, it has been opened by one of the name of MaK Lairen.*"

This was quite extraordinary, for Captain MacLaren and Garrick were together at the hotel when the letter arrived. Garrick had asked Capt. MacLaren to open it as he was busy.

The letter continued:

> "*But as to the box—some say tin. This they will find not one hundred yards from the spot.* Can the box be seen? *The tin is quite visible though snow is falling.* Where exactly is it? *It is near the Coire Achallander[1] and if they are quick they will find it . . . The stream of the corrie starting at Ford. Yes, you will follow the corrie, or some say coire, and it goes to the bogland at altitude already mentioned— 3060 feet. Yes, it is a burn, though the word is new to me. I regret my gernadion* (messenger?—author) *is no longer here; but from the report delivered the news is on climbing the korrie, or I believe corrie. I noticed a box I think he called it, and a*

---

[1] This is the old spelling of the name.

kloot of linen. The word of the gernadion is in Scots and represents box-mullie. What is a mullie? *I am sorry my Scots is so poor[2], it is new to me. The gernadion spoke of the box as a mull-lie, that is, a little mull[3]. The contents of the box is linen and it is stiff with batter[4]... To climb the corrie is easy—it is commonly used by—help me with this—Gillies—pronounced gilly... The snow fall increases and I fear that many little clues will be obliterated. One thing remains that it is about altitude 3060 feet that the find will be made."*

The letter concluded that no harm could be done by trying to verify the directions given, and was again signed "STILL ANXIOUS TO HELP".

The fifth and final letter, postmarked Peterhead, 6th April, arrived on the 7th at the Royal Hotel and read:

"Dear Sir, I am sorry we have not much to give you but it may be of interest to the 'speculators'. (The letters were causing much controversy. Many of the searchers were sceptical—author). 3 p.m. Sat. *I say they have read your letter and whilst laughing in their faces I should say it is not in their hearts—they say, What of this? Who is this?* Sat. 9 p.m. *My last advice is to take the corrie at Achallander House... and at altitude given, and to the north you should encounter your object. There is a dark, stone ridge— I forget the technical name—at or near the* spot. Is there a precipice? *Yes, it is a precipice. I think MaK Lairen said heugh or kleugh...* 11 p.m. Have they got the rough map I sent them? *Yes, they say it is a copy of a map.* Can they make anything of it? *Yes, it is quite intelligible to them.* (Doubts about the letters had arisen because the searchers had carbon-copied the sketches and then read the reverse tracing in error—author). Mon 4 p.m. *The letters have caused much comment and some heed is being paid. Two of the company believe your good faith—one is called Walker. Stewart says 'I know no-one in Peterhead'."* (These were Robert Stewart's precise words on opening the fourth letter—author).

The letter was signed for the last time, "STILL ANXIOUS TO HELP".

The searchers, now realising they had made a mistake over the sketches, decided to follow the directions and clues given in the letters as all else had failed. The last major search was organised for Sunday, 13th April, exactly three weeks after Henderson went missing. In the afternoon the farmer of Achallader, Duncan Smith, found the body of Alexander Henderson lying face down on a shallow slope in the north-west corrie where the mysterious sketches had shown him to be.

He had no broken bones, but had a deep wound on his forehead. It appeared he had slipped, and either struck his head on his ice-axe or a rock. He had then slithered unconscious downhill for 150 feet until stopped by a boulder at precisely the altitude of 3060 feet where the first letters stated he would be.

His rucksack was still on his back, but his vacuum flask was broken and protruded through the fabric. Many thought that this was the mull or box with a linen kloot. However, the letters stated that this small

---

[2] Sir Arthur Conan Doyle who investigated this case, believed that the gernadion was an old Greek who had learned Scots from another spirit.

[3] Mull is an old Scots word for a type of snuff box.

[4] Probably cardboard.

The Royal Hotel, Tyndrum. It was here that the mysterious letters arrived giving information on the lost climbers.

tin box was visible some distance from the body, and *contained* stiff linen. This may have been a cloth-backed map inside a waterproof tin, and was probably dropped 150 feet above, where his ice-axe was later found.

His body was carried down to Bridge of Orchy church, then home to Cupar for burial.

Now that it was seen that all the clues given in the letters appeared to tie in precisely with events, the identity of the writer began to provoke much interest. An astute reporter from the *Dundee Advertiser* eventually tracked him down as one Norman MacDiarmid, a gentleman in his late thirties who had lived at Killin before the Great War, and was of independent means. He had purchased Buchan Ness Lodge at Boddam in Aberdeenshire in 1920, and wrote articles on natural history for various journals. He was known locally as somewhat of a recluse.

The reporter questioned him for several hours, but MacDiarmid refused to answer anything about the letters. The reporter then managed to locate a friend of MacDiarmid's, described as occupying a position of high standing in Peterhead. The friend told him that, just for a laugh, a few of them had started seances some months previously. It was during these that they realised MacDiarmid possessed a hitherto unknown gift as a medium. On numerous occasions he would suddenly start writing backwards at high speed.

They had first realised he appeared to be receiving messages from an unknown, higher source, when he had drawn a sketch of a large car and a small car with the word "me" beside it. This was immediately followed by a name and address in Musselburgh. They had all been stunned to read in the next day's paper that a boy of that name and address had been killed in a road accident in that town about the time MacDiarmid had drawn his sketch.

However, on the night the first Achallader letter had been written, there had been a social gathering in the friend's house attended by his wife and daughter, two friends and MacDiarmid. They had all been laughing and joking when MacDiarmid began to write backwards automatically, and it was only after this had been held to a mirror that the group realised it might have something to do with the reported disappearance of Alexander Henderson on distant Ben Achallader. MacDiarmid's friend, who remains unnamed to this day, had copied the messages into the letters, and sent them on just in case they were of any assistance. The group of six then tried to help MacDiarmid to obtain further information from his unknown source over the next three weeks.

Unfortunately, the Achallader Letters were destroyed when the Royal Hotel burned down in 1931. The proprietor, Robert Stewart, died two years later.

Norman MacDiarmid seems to have worked in the Glasgow docks after the last War, returning each night to a cottage near Stirling where he lived the life of a recluse. He was extremely shy, refusing all invitations to lecture on his gift, and I have been unable to find out if he ever received any more such messages from his spirit source.

The case is still baffling. Was it all coincidence? Was Henderson still alive four days after his disappearance as the first letter seemed to imply. Could he have been saved if the letters had been believed and their directions followed? Is there indeed a spirit world which is able through mediums such as Norman MacDiarmid to make vague contact with the living?

I wonder . . . ◪

ELECTRIC BRAE—THE SHOCKING TRUTH

Ken Andrew

For those who don't know about it, The Electric Brae on the A719 in Ayrshire comes as a unique surprise. Unless its "magic" is allowed to work on them, though, and the reasons considered, its name may signify nothing, and road users will traverse it ignorant of its claim to fame.

Approaching from the north, motorists enjoy a magnificent view of Culzean Bay. "SLOW", painted in white on the road, calls their attention to the foreground before they drive round the left-hand bend to come across a sign stating mysteriously—

CROY BRAE
ELECTRIC BRAE

E

No crackle will disturb car radios, no electrified fences will threaten, no pylons dominate, no power stations are visible and no lodestone or ley line will exert any influence.

Yet the brae seems to behave in an extraordinary way. As you drive "down" it, the car will slow and demand more acceleration. If you drive "up", the car starts to run away and you have to slacken speed.

Correspondence in *The Scots Magazine* during 1986 attributed this effect to the earth's energy system—an unseen world "which science cannot at present touch". According to the writer, he experienced "the most powerful energy anomaly I have ever encountered" on the Electric Brae, and he linked this with the idea of ley lines and the power displayed by poltergeists in moving objects.

Since the early 1940s I have travelled Croy Brae, and I have never heard such theories, or anyone else disputing the accepted explanation for the Electric Brae—that it is merely an optical illusion.

To settle the issue once and for all, I set out to do some investigations.

The 1:50000 O.S. map shows a spot height of 75 metres some distance north of the brae. The road then rises over one contour to meet another at the west end of the brae, continues along the contour line to the burn at the east end of the brae, then bends to the south to a spot height of 87 metres near Knoweside.

The road has thus risen 12 metres over a mile, but ups and downs along that distance, including the crucial quarter-mile slope of Croy Brae, cannot be readily determined in the small detail.

The 25-inch map of 1856 settles the matter conclusively. The road coming from the north rises in feet from spot heights of 266, 273 and 282 to 286 at the start of the brae at the west end. A bench mark of 294.8 feet is given on a milestone about one quarter of the way along the brae going east. A spot height of 299 feet is recorded west of the Croy Burn at the east end of the brae.

Southbound travellers therefore have to climb about 13 feet between the signposts that denote the Electric Brae today. Northbound travellers turn westwards into the brae and drop 13 feet. That is not the impression they will have, however, for the eastward travellers imagine they are descending while those west-bound think they are climbing!

The 1856 map does not mention the words Croy Brae or Electric Brae so probably the phenomenon was not widely known until the advent of the car. Knoweside Farm and cottages east of the Croy Burn are shown on the 1856 map. These, or others on the site, and the milestone, are still present today.

As a preliminary to some simple experiments on the brae's mysterious "powers" I stepped out the distance between the signposts at either end. From the west sign it was 220 paces to the start of the lay-by, which extends for 35 paces, and a further 145 paces took me to the east sign— making the brae 400 paces long.

It was a quiet day, with little traffic, so I did some test drives. First of all I made three runs west to east at 20, 30 and 40 mph and three east to west at the same speeds—allowing my car to freewheel from those speeds as soon as I reached the first of the signs.

Going from the west at 20 mph and apparently travelling downhill, the car stopped after 81 paces. At 30 mph my speed was down to 3 mph at 220 paces and I was stationary soon after. At 40 mph, my speed was sufficient to allow me to complete the brae doing 10 mph.

Travelling west, and apparently uphill, I

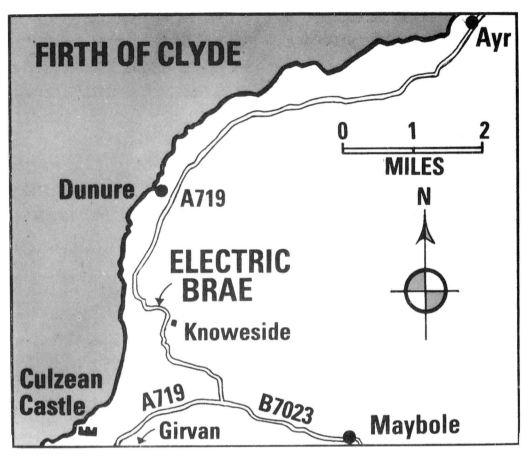

freewheeled from a start of 20 mph and reached the end of the brae doing 2 mph. From 30 I was rolling comfortably past the end of the brae at 15 mph. From 40, I reached the end doing 26 mph.

The slope was obviously not steep enough to counter the effect of friction between the road surface and my tyres. Had it been longer, I would have come to a standstill in either direction, even starting from 40 mph. Travelling westwards was definitely easier, though it appeared to be uphill, and in none of my three tests in that direction had the slope stopped me. Travelling east, and apparently downhill, I had slowed quickly, and could not manage the brae at speeds of 30 mph or less.

The appearance of hedges and fences climbing in both directions from a low point at the lay-by must undoubtedly help to create the illusion concerning the brae.

Travelling south, motorists turn eastwards into the brae round the end of the Carrick Hills. Culzean, caravan sites, arable fields, buildings and sea-level are to the front and right. The high, rough ground of the hills has been passed and motorists are conditioned into thinking they are now going downhill. The relationship between Croy Brae and its surroundings is masked by the bend and a belt of beech, ash and sycamore running down the glen of the Croy Burn beyond the eastern sign. With the hedges rising higher on either side the road appears to be descending when it is really rising slightly.

North-bound travellers are similarly fooled. As they drop from 440 to 287 feet just south of Knoweside Farm, they are being conditioned for the hidden brae ahead. The road to the shore falls away at an angle behind on the left, Knoweside sits above on the right, the wooded glen of the Croy Burn rises steeply in front with the slopes of Bennan Hill rearing higher on the left. Everything suggests that the way forward must be upwards.

There is a little dip just north of Knoweside and then the road very definitely starts to climb (17 feet on the 1856 map) to Craigencroy Toll at the bend. Here the trees shut out the surroundings. As cars leave the trees they pass the first Electric Brae sign and there is no view west to Arran as might be expected. Instead, the ridge of Bennan Hill slopes down from the right in front of the road, suggesting an imminent ascent. The effect is reinforced by the rising hedges and fences beyond the lay-by. In fact, of course, the road is falling, and rounds the ridge with a slight curve to the left starting at the lay-by.

All this becomes clearer if you walk the brae or leave the road and view the area from ground to the east and south. Between Knoweside Hill and Castlehill Wood, the horizon of the Firth of Clyde can be used as a level to gauge the true tendency of the road and its real relationship with the landscape.

As already shown, the slope up or down is not dramatic, with a gradient of only about 1 in 90. Motorists seeking to test the brae's unique effect may sometimes need to persevere to find the right spots where vehicles will appear to defy gravity—especially if tyre pressures are too low. In some parts of the brae, a vehicle can sit still and may not roll easily in any direction.

The brae can be very busy at times, especially in summer, when tour buses and cars are trying out its alleged powers. Patience is called for by those in a hurry or used to the experience.

It would be interesting to learn who first called it the "Electric Brae". It does not appear on the Popular Edition one-inch map of 1945, but before that date I can recall being introduced to the brae and its curious effect in my father's car.

The brae was much enjoyed by US personnel serving at Prestwick Airport from the Forties on. New arrivals from across the Atlantic were rushed to see it at the first opportunity, and if dollars could have bought it, we would have lost it by now. General Eisenhower was most intrigued by the brae and brought visitors to see it from his flat at Culzean. At one time, Ayr County Council was receiving so many enquiries that it issued a special descriptive leaflet.

Behind the apparently magical effects, science has a simple and prosaic explanation for the phenomenon, and it has nothing to do with electricity or unknown forces working along mysterious lines.

I am sorry if I disappoint some of my readers, but the brae is simply an optical illusion, though interesting enough on that account and certainly well worth a visit.

CUSTOMS

IT'S THE BURRY MAN'S DAY!

Dorothy K. Haynes visited South Queensferry when the little
Royal Burgh celebrated this colourful annual tradition.

With a crowd of children tagging behind, I followed the Burry Man round the streets of South Queensferry. He was a strange sight, a grotesque sight; covered completely in green burrs, his head decorated with flowers, he lumbered stiffly along, his outstretched hands grasping flower-decked poles for support.

No one could tell me how or when the custom originated. My landlady had a theory, gathered from uncertain sources! "They say it was a man who was ship-wrecked and had no clothes, so he dressed himself in burrs."

It seemed a heroic, but improbable story, and nobody else agreed.

"Och, no. It's a fertility rite."

"Something to do with Covenanters escaping. Camouflage and all that." But the Burry Man existed before Covenanting days.

"I think it's a thanksgiving for the harvest."

Early August seems a bit premature for that.

Some other guesses are that it may have something to do with, variously, the Lammas Fair, the Barn Man, the Spirit of Vegetation, nature worship, the Leaf Man of Central Europe, and England's Jack in the Green. Some Morris dancers wear a badge portraying something like the Burry Man. Yet another theory is that he is a sort of scapegoat, taking on himself all the sins of the people and carrying them away.

The question was clinched by a man who said to me, in a once-and-for-all tone, "Well, Sir Walter Scott tried to find out aboot him, and *he* couldnae dae it, so . . ."

Whatever his origin, the Burry Man has been making his walk annually for hundreds of years. Queensferry, a Royal Burgh with a charter conferred by David II, has had a Ferry Fair from the 15th century, an old-fashioned fair, always on a Saturday, at which stalls sold gingerbread and other goodies in the streets. Long ago it used to be held in June, but the date was unsuitable for the Burry Man to have his festival the day before. The burrs which he wears come from the burdock plant, which does not produce burrs in June, so the Fair and the Burry Man's Day reverted to August.

Today, of course, a street market is out of the question; Queensferry has traffic problems enough without that! But the Fair goes on and, like many other Scottish towns, Queensferry has adopted the custom of crowning an annual queen. The first Ferry Queen was crowned in 1926.

This year, everyone said, there was greater enthusiasm than there had been for some time. Flags were up, and the entrances to the homes of the Queen and her ladies-in-waiting were decorated with evergreens and floral archways. I passed one garden in which a monster toadstool and fairy figures were floodlit at night.

However, before the Queen came the Burry Man.

I made a point of meeting him while he was still recognisable. Alan Reid, now doing his fifth year as Burry Man, is an oil rig worker in Norway, and an amateur boxer of some standing. He looks fit; he would have to be. A Burry Man can lose up to 7 lbs after his gruelling day.

Intrigued, I asked him if anyone can be a Burry Man.

"Yes, if he's a native of Queensferry." (The term for that is a "Bellstane Bird.")

"How is he chosen?"

"Well, there's a committee, but you volunteer."

"Do they get many volunteers?"

"Not really. That's why I took it on again. I wouldn't like to see it fading out. So if nobody else was going to do it, I said I'd have another go. It's only one day in the year."

"What do you think about it?" I asked his wife.

"I'm quite proud that he does it."

Civic pride comes into it; but few central figures of civic festivals have to endure such an ordeal.

"Apart from keeping it going, what do you get out of it, then?"

"Well, there's kids going round with collecting boxes all day, but if anyone tells you I'm making a bomb, don't you believe it. To begin with, the clothes I wear are ruined; I pay the dressers, and the collectors get their whack; and, if I take time off work, that's to be made up, too."

It must be at least as hard a day as any he spends on the oil rig. He is on the go from nine in the morning till six at night, but his day starts even earlier than that. It takes three hours to dress him.

I turned up when the dressing was nearly complete. It was just before nine o'clock and he'd been getting ready since about six. A less dedicated person would have given up long ago.

I had seen photographs of former Burry Men, so I knew what to expect, but, even so, I was startled when I saw him. Legs apart, hands outstretched, he looked like a figure in green chain mail. His hat was decked with fresh roses, he had roses on his shoulders and stuck into the Union Jack which girded his waist. Burrs hid his face and body. Only an arm was still visible, and patches of cloth covered in burrs lay ready to be pressed on. I was allowed to apply one of these patches, and ex-provost Milne applied another. When the cloth is peeled off, the burrs stick to the woollen jersey below.

The men who were dressing him were deft and experienced. Walter Quigley is a veteran at the job, and has spare patches ready in case any of the burrs work loose. Helping also were the Burry Man's assistants, his brother Colin and cousin Bert Magain. These two were to walk beside him, one on each side, guiding him, because he is virtually blind behind his prickly mask. They hold the staves which the Burry Man grasps to support his arms. These staves are decorated with sheaves of flowers, roses, lilies, buddleia and other bright and fragrant blooms.

I hoped that Alan had had a good breakfast, because he would not be able to eat all day. Nor could he take anything to drink, except the various statutory drams, and even these would have to be sucked through a straw. He couldn't possibly get anything to his lips. "It's got to be whisky," he told me the night before. "Whisky dries you up. I couldn't take a long drink like beer, because I can't go to the toilet."

A last smoke. A last check on the patches, and a few extra burrs pressed into place, and it was time to go.

Walking is awkward. The costume is unbelievably heavy and he can't bend his legs, so going down the stairs is a chancy business. Wide-legged, grasping his staves, Alan headed his following of children along the High Street, Hopetoun Road and into Villa Road, where he got his first dram from the Provost. South Queensferry, a Royal Burgh, retains its provost's chain of office, which ex-Provost Milne, now a District Councillor, wears on civic occasions. The provost's lamp is still at the gate, surmounted by a naval crown.

Off again, with the children ringing a bell and cheering and running ahead with collecting boxes, halting cars, knocking at every door. We went into the housing schemes, and mothers held up children to see the sight. Some of them, newcomers to the village, were obviously puzzled by the strange apparition. Cameras clicked all the way. A few girls posed for photographs with the Burry Man, but refused a kiss! I found myself stopping to enlighten the curious. I was glad of the chance now and then to lag a little and then sprint to make up time. Walking at about one mile per hour is more tiring than a brisk stride and it is only too easy to drop into the Burry Man's rocking shuffle.

Hip, hip hooray!
It's the Burry Man's Day!

More and more children joined us. Only a few of the tiny ones seemed afraid of the groping green figure. No doubt they see much worse on television. I was inclined to feel that there was something pathetic about him, but in horror films I always feel sorry for the monsters.

At St Margaret's School, we stopped to meet two distinguished guests, the Lord Provost of Edinburgh and Tam Dalyell, MP. This was the first time either had visited the Burry Man festival, and the Lord Provost looked as if he couldn't really believe it. Bees were buzzing round the roses on the Burry Man's hat, which alone had taken three hours to decorate.

A voice from the burry green face explained to the visitors that he entered people's houses when invited, and that some old people would have thought it unlucky if he didn't come in. The collectors rattled their cans, the distinguished visitors contributed cheerfully, and drove away, amused, but impressed.

I found myself tending to address the attendants when I wanted to know anything, rather than the Burry Man himself. I had to remind myself that he was perfectly capable of hearing and answering. It was a reminder that you are very likely to do the same with disabled people, forgetting that they are neither deaf nor unable to answer for themselves.

Next we went to the huge Hewlett Packard factory, causing some consternation at the desk, where the receptionist was new, and apparently unaware of the weird local custom. Luckily, there was a lift large enough for the Burry Man and his entourage. We stood in the canteen; more photographs and stares, and a good deal of laughter, then another dram, and we made off to an inn in the housing scheme, with a following now of snazzy new bikes, several excited dogs, and the bell clanging all the way. Here the collectors, who had worked like Trojans, were to have refreshments. Having neither the Burry Man's stamina nor his restriction on nourishment, I made off myself and went to the Queensferry Arms for lunch.

When I came out, there was no sign of the shambling green figure, so I took the chance of a look round the sunlit village. I visited the Priory, an old Carmelite church, and sat in its beautiful garden overlooking the firth. Sails were out on the pale blue

Alan Reid, the South Queensferry Burry Man in 1982, presents a strange sight covered from head to toe in thistle burrs. Dorothy Haynes explains this ancient custom.

PHOTO: HARRY KELLY

water. Here it was that Queen Margaret, wife of William Canmore, crossed in the Royal ferry going to and from Edinburgh; indeed the burgh coat of arms incorporates a figure of the Queen standing up in a tiny boat in a fashion calculated to coup it at any minute into the rocking waters.

Now the two great bridges rival each other, reaching across to Fife. Queensferry is dominated by the Forth bridges, and they never look alike from one day to another, their colour and perspective changing with the weather and the light.

At four o'clock I met up again with the Burry Man, trudging down the Loan towards the Vat 69 distillery as the workers were coming out. More money for the cans! After this, we lumbered through the town to where a fair was opening up for the evening beside the Hawes Inn. A long pause here for a rest and a dram, then a slow progress back the way, with a drink at every pub—about ten of them! Colin Reid, the Burry Man's brother, who is almost T T, confessed that he felt rather out of it with the occasional half pint of shandy.

The flowers on the staves were wilted now, the splendid blooms on the hat drooping and half their size. A rose fell to the ground. The Burry Man's feet were dragging and he even staggered a little towards the end of his travels. His escort, however, rejected any suggestion that the drams might be responsible. "He's tired," he said, and I believed him. He had covered about nine arduous miles.

I was there when the costume came off. First the hat. "Feel that," said Colin. I judged it to weigh about seven pounds. Next, the burrs were picked quickly from his face, then the mask and Balaclava helmet were peeled over his head, rather an agonising experience. "How do you feel?" I asked as Alan emerged.

"Hot," he said briefly. He looked hot; he also looked quite sober!

They passed me the burry pullover to feel. It, too, was unbelievably heavy, and there were still the trousers to come. I left them to it. The hat, with its decorations, was to go to the Queen's Retreat bar, at the cost of £1, and the Burry Man would probably have a good meal and a night out. He had certainly earned it.

After tea, the Fair festivities took over. There was a pram race, with a pint to be consumed at every stopping place; later on came two boundary races, on cycle and on foot and an up-to-the-minute item, a skateboard slalom. Two greasy poles were erected for climbing, an old Ferry tradition. The prize used to be a ham, but now the winner is awarded money for reaching the top. Last year, I was told, a girl entered for the first time—and won! This year the first contestant reached the top right away, so there wasn't much competition after that. Perhaps next year the pole will have to be twice as high and even greasier.

To finish off, there was a fancy dress competition, at which last year's Queen presented the prizes. Everything was set fair for the coronation in the morning.

Alas, in the morning it rained solid, drenching rain that sparked off the pavements and hid the bridges in mist. The crowds gathering in the street, and on the railed terraces above the shops, shook their heads under their umbrellas as the water ran into their shoes. "We don't seem to get a right forecast ataa. They said it would be fine."

"I could have telt ye," said an older man behind me. "When ye can hear trains on the bridge at night, ye ken it'll rain in the morning."

Oddly enough, I had heard the trains almost too clearly to be able to sleep; but I thought it had meant *good* weather.

There was talk of the procession being cancelled, but the children themselves decided to carry on. A pipe band went past, a pageant of Children of the World, two decorated floats, a troupe of white-clad majorettes, and then the court, in cars.

They were a beautifully-trained court, the ladies-in-waiting in twos in different-coloured dresses, the boys in kilts and white shirts. The Queen, royally dis-

regarding the rain, knelt to be crowned by Mrs Young, a lady just due to retire as school swimming instructress. (The children, she said, were more familiar to her dripping wet and they were becoming more recognisable every minute!)

An interesting point was that this year's queen was to be crowned with the "old" crown. Last year's, I was told, was a "beauty queen's crown." Looking at former photographs, I agree that this year's choice was the right one. It set off a very charming and composed queen. The bearing of everyone on the platform, including the clear-voiced herald, who delivered his speech beautifully, but didn't quite synchronise his trumpet with the fanfare offstage, was as dignified as that of the Lanimer Queen's court, and what higher praise can a Lanarkian give?

The day should have been a washout—it was the wettest on record—but it wasn't. Drenched and dripping, with my feet in a puddle and my hands slipping on the wet railing of the terrace, I saw the scene as one of both dignity and gaiety. Rainwear isn't drab these days. Bright umbrellas made the street look Continental, and the stage had a backing of real roses and hydrangeas. The crowd, too, were not in the least despondent, apart from the reiterated commiseration, "It's the kiddies I'm sorry for." The people of Queensferry—the "Ferry Folk"—are the friendliest ever. They all spoke to me as if I'd known them for years.

The Queen's bouquet was laid on the War Memorial, and the children went off for bags of buns and what-nots. The rest of the festivities were deferred till the middle of the week.

It was time for me to go. After waiting 20 minutes at Waverley Station for a ticket, it was good to be served immediately at Dalmeny (the station for South Queensferry), and to receive, unasked for, a brisk summary of my trains from Edinburgh to Glasgow, complete with platform numbers. All part of the Ferry service?

I didn't see the Burry Man again. No doubt he was sleeping it off after a day's mortification and a night's celebration. I hope he brought luck and a prosperous year to the Ferry and its inhabitants, and I hope his collecting tins were full. He earned every penny! ⚐

WHAT THEY READ THEN

The general convention of the Royal Burrows of this Kingdom having appointed the members for the Burrows of Edinburgh, Perth, Dundee, Aberdeen, Stirling, Linlithgow, St Andrews, Glasgow and Inverbervy, as a committee of their number, to wait on the Duke of Argyle, to assure him of the great regard they have for his Grace's person and family, and to declare their entire satisfaction with his Grace's appearances for the honour and interest of his Majesty, the preservation of the liberties of his Majesty's subjects, the commerce of the nation, the rights and privileges of the Royal Burrows, and the city of Edinburgh in particular; the committee accordingly waited upon his Grace, and the Lord Provost of

Edinburgh, July 4.

Edinburgh, as Preses, having addressed his Grace, with great eloquence, to the purpose of above mentioned, his Grace answered, "I am unworthy of the great honour the Royal Burrows are pleased to do me. I have, in all my actions, most sincerely meant the service of my King and country. It was my indispensible duty so to do. Merit I have done."

Since our last the *May* and *Anne*, Captain Robert Angus, cleared out of Leith for London, with the following Scots manufacturers, biz. 18,750 yards linen, 1850 yards tartan, 2450 pounds thread and yarn, 647 dozen linen handkerchiefs, 2686 dozen skins.

From *The Scots Magazine*, June 1740.

CHARACTERS AND PERSONALITIES

THE MAN WHO HATED SIXPENCES

Margaret MacDougall tells the moving, true story of the tragic figure behind Scott's famous fictional character, The Black Dwarf.

David Ritchie, second son of a slate-quarry labourer, was born about 1740 in the parish of Stobo, Peebles-shire. He was never to grow more than 40 inches high, and his misshapen legs ended in fin-like feet which he wrapped in cloth. He never wore shoes, and got around by poling himself along with a staff, considerably longer than himself.

His father said of him: "He was born either to slay or be slain." The sense of his deformity, said another contemporary, "haunted him like a phantom".

Many years later, Dr John Brown, author of *Rab and his Friends*, looking clinically at the cruelly-twisted leg bones, commented that merely to see them—and add poverty—was to know the misery summed up in their possession. It was a harsh sentence to bear through a long life (Davie lived to be over 70), especially in an age when there was much ignorance and little sympathy for physical deformity.

Young Davie made a brave enough start, setting off for Edinburgh to learn the trade of a brush-maker. His extraordinary appearance attracted so much attention from what he termed "keelies" that he retreated to his native hills like a wounded animal. It was the first of many slights and rebuffs.

His was going to be a life lived mainly on the charity of others, the parish where he was born bearing some responsibility. Davie had moved with his parents from Stobo to Manor, but after their early

Davie Ritchie, the dwarf whose deformities 'haunted him like a phantom'. He poled himself along as he couldn't walk on his heavily bandaged feet.

Davie's cottage at Woodhouse, photographed late last century. He shared it with his sister. She had her own door while Davie's shuttered window gave him the absolute privacy he craved.

PHOTO: TWEEDDALE DISTRICT MUSEUMS

deaths, he went back over the hills three times to make a claim on his native parish.

The first time was on Communion Monday, 26th August 1771, when he was presented with a sixpence. Two years later he made the arduous (for him) journey again, and received another sixpence. As well as inducing a life-long antipathy to sixpences, the stingy treatment so incensed him that he stayed away for nine years. When he came back in 1782, his reward was a shilling. After that, he never returned.

It then fell to the farming community of Manor to support him. The dwarf's meal-pock hung at the local mill for a contribution from everyone who had a melder ground. He went the rounds of the local farms, staying a week or two in each, earning his keep by telling stories, and ignoring, as best he could, the giggling farm servants.

He clutched his pride about him, and it was said "counted it no small honour conferred, by giving them the favour of his company". His pride must have been difficult to sustain, though, for the hospitality was always on the farmer's terms.

For instance, Newby was a favourite port of call, and Mrs Gibson, the farmer's wife, was always kind to him. However, when Davie arrived one day, his usual bed was not available as "more gentle" visitors had arrived. Davie was directed to the hay loft.

The next morning a farm servant, on her way to milk the ewes, spotted Davie perched up a tree where he had spent the night. He told her he had preferred the tree to her mistress's hospitality, and he never totally forgot or forgave their indifference.

Other insights into his psychological sufferings are to be found in excerpts from the journal which he kept and which was discovered in his cottage after his death. Although he had little formal education, Davie could read and write, and enjoyed both poetry and history.

He recorded that one Handsel Monday when he had poled himself the four miles to Peebles to see his friend James Ritchie, they had a good-going discussion on the subject of the rotation of the earth. "He was clean against it," wrote Davie. "I was for it."

The pleasure of the day was destroyed when he was followed on his way home "by some damned brush* as if I had been a world's wonder". He could happily have poured "seething lead" down through them (a favourite thought he often had for punishing those who mocked him). "Hell will never be fou till they are in it," he added.

In spite of his deformity he found a lass willing to marry him, and went several times to the manse to ask the minister to perform the ceremony. The man finally sent him away, saying he neither could nor would marry him.

According to the account of Robert Craig, a surgeon in Peebles at the time, the dwarf swung himself out of the door on his pole, banging the door behind him in anger. He then opened it again, shook his clenched fist at the minister's face, and exploded, "Weel, weel, ye'll no let decent, honest folk marry; but I'll plenish your parish wi bastards, so see what ye'll mak o that!" How the tongues must have clacked over that encounter.

No-one seems to have considered Davie

---

* Brush seems to have been Davie's equivalent of trash.

ill done-by over the issue. The lass was considered to be haverill (half-witted). Little wonder Davie had a reputation for a black temper and was given to demonstrating the strength of his skull by striking it through the panel of a door or the bottom of a barrel.

However great his local notoriety, if a certain young man had not one day come to visit him in his cottage, Davie would now be lying forgotten in his grave at Manor kirkyard.

In 1797, the dwarf's near neighbour, Dr Adam Ferguson of Hallyards (who sometimes loaned Davie books from his library), brought the young Walter Scott to the stone and turf cottage. Describing the encounter, Dr Robert Chambers, writer and publisher, said the lameness of the stranger lessened the gulf there was with most other visitors.

Scott was greatly impressed by Davie's spirit. Years later he immortalised him in the character of Elshender, the misanthropic Black Dwarf in *Tales of My Landlord*.

Was he fair to the real Davie? In Peebles, even to this day, it is the Black Dwarf image which prevails. There are some in the town who remember being threatened as children with the Black Dwarf if they did not get to sleep. Yet Miss Ballantyne of Woodhouse who knew the real man said he was especially kind to children.

At this distance in time it is difficult to discover the real Bow'd Davie o the Wuddus (Woodhouse), as he was known then. Peebles Museum has his garden trowel in a glass case, but no-one in the museum can say what happened to his curious journal.

At Hallyards there is a statue of the Black Dwarf, one of a series of Scott characters made by Forrest of Leith. It took seven horses to cart it over the Meldons, to where it stands at Hallyards like a refugee from Disneyland. No sign

This statue of Scott's character The Black Dwarf stands in the grounds of Hallyards. Visitors to the Manor Valley can see the sculpture, but should call first at the house by the main gate.

PHOTO: TWEEDDALE DISTRICT COUNCIL

here of the terrible malformations that made Mungo Park compare the legs to a pair of corkscrews. While a surgeon in Peebles, he operated on Davie Ritchie for a strangulated hernia.

At Woodhouse there is the cottage in which Davie spent his last nine years. He shared it with his sister, on condition that she had her own door and left him severely alone. His sister was not physically deformed, but suffered from some degree of mental retardation which must have made her poor company for his quick mind.

This was his second cottage in the same area. The first one he built mainly by his own efforts (and, some said, without even asking the permission of the local land-owner.) He surrounded it with a wall and dug himself a garden, using a special spade which he could force down with his chest.

Davie's garden outshone the kailyards of his neighbours, for the dwarf loved plants. He also kept bees, fruit trees and rowans (to ward off witches, for he was exceedingly superstitious), and grew herbs and vegetables.

His bees and vegetables gave him enough income to keep him in snuff at least. For company he had a cat and a dog, and as they never teased him about his appearance, he was devoted to them.

When I visited the dwarf's cottage, there, beside his sister's normal-sized door was the little one which he had insisted on for himself. There, too, was his small window with the wooden shutter, for he

The Black Dwarf's cottage as it is today, complete with Davie's low door and shuttered window.

PHOTO: MARGARET MACDOUGALL

refused to allow glass. He needed, it seemed, to be able to keep out the world entirely.

Here in 1811 Mrs Ballantyne was hastily summoned from nearby Woodhouse having been told that it was "just about a owre wi Davie noo". She went, and Davie breathed his last almost immediately. The good lady was rather shocked at the speed with which his sister, feeble-brained or not, got the dwarf's keys and opened his secret repository. Inside were three money bags, containing £22 made up of every variety of coin, except, of course, sixpences.

Davie Ritchie had often expressed the wish to be buried on the top of Woodhill, with a planting of rowans beside him. He

The Black Dwarf's gravestone. It was provided by the Chambers brothers of Peebles 30 years after his death.

PHOTO: TWEEDDALE DISTRICT COUNCIL

did not want to be buried in Manor kirkyard "among the common brush," nor did he want the clods clapped down on him "by such a fellow as Jock Somerville, the bellman"—further examples of Davie's pride even in death.

He had never been a kirk attender, a fact which made some people suspect him of unorthodox beliefs. The explanation was simpler: he disliked the public scrutiny which churchgoing would have entailed. Perhaps, too, the minister's refusal to perform the marriage ceremony had something to do with it.

Alas for poor Davie, his friend, Sir James Nasmyth, the local landowner who had promised to honour his burial wish, was out of the country at the time of his death. The dwarf was buried in the kirkyard after all, and probably with the despised bellman in attendance. He did at least eventually get one rowan, for 30 years later the Chambers brothers of Peebles marked the grave with an impressive headstone—and a rowan tree.

Even in death poor Davie was not left in peace. A rumour had spread that his body had been lifted and taken to Glasgow for dissection. When his sister died in 1821, the grave-diggers took the opportunity to check if there was any truth in the rumour. Yet another indignity ensued, for although the skeleton was found to be there, it was removed from the specially-deep coffin which had been made to accommodate the twisted limbs. The remains were taken to Woodhouse, and the leg-bones kept when the rest of the skeleton was re-interred.

The bones came into the possession of Dr John Brown who wrote that he had been given them by Andrew Ballantyne of Woodhouse. A woodcut illustration of them appears in Brown's *Horae Subsecivae*. Where the bones are now, I have not discovered.

The ruins of the cottage at Torroble in Sutherland where Big Sam MacDonald was born in 1762.

J. L. GOSKIRK

ABOVE: Drummietermont Farm and the field in which Miss Smith saw the vision of the Picts after the Battle of Nechtanesmere.   JOHN RUNDLE

BELOW: Kinloch Castle on Rum. Archie Cameron's memories of the Castle and the Bullough family who owned it make fascinating reading.   NATIONAL TRUST FOR SCOTLAND

ABOVE: The Island of Dun in the St Kilda group where Rennie McOwan spent the night.

BELOW: Altnaharra with Ben Klibreck behind. This was the starting point for Tom Weir's 'Remotest North' walking holiday.

ABOVE: Puffins at Kearvaig Bay were one of the delights of Tom Weir's Sutherland exploration in 1949.
TOM WEIR

RIGHT: Handa Island and the distant Sutherland mountains. A scene unchanged for thousands of years.
TOM WEIR

Martin Moran – the first person to complete a continuous ascent of all our Munros in winter.

ABOVE: Are you looking uphill or downhill? See Ken Andrew's chapter 'The Shocking Truth' about Ayrshire's famous Electric Brae.   KEN ANDREW

BELOW: Glasgow's Kelvingrove Art Gallery. Popular folklore says it was built back to front by mistake, but this is just one of many apocryphal stories circulating today – see Gordon McCulloch's article.   VAL BISSLAND

ABOVE: Rowan berries form a substantial part of the pine marten's diet as Lea MacNally discloses in his article 'Up at the Martens'.   LEA MACNALLY

BELOW: Willie Bernard at the memorial stone to the climbers Barrie and Baird.   W. D. BERNARD

How shall we remember Davie?

In a book published in 1820, *The Life and Anecdotes of the Black Dwarf or David Ritchie* there is the following epitaph:

*Here lies the wond'rous Dwarf of
    Manor's glen,*
*Transfix'd at last with Death's all-
    lev'lling dart;*
*In death alone was he like other
    men,*
*In life he always bore a diff'rent
    part;*
*Light lies the turf upon the
    wither'd heart,*
*Which never felt the balm of
    sympathy;*
A creature of another kind, a start
*From Nature's chain, whose dire
    misanthropy*
*Found only refuge when it found
    that bliss—to die.*

Somehow that epitaph seems inappropriate for the real Davie, poling himself determinedly to Peebles and back in order to enjoy a crack with his friends. Of course he had a black temper, but given his deformities and the treatment he received, who could blame him? He was also a man who loved flowers, the Border landscape, the poetry of Allan Ramsay, the company of animals, beautiful women, and children (if they did not tease).

For an epitaph I prefer the words of Nannie Ritchie (no relation as far as I can tell), whose parents often gave hospitality to Davie on his visits to Peebles. Asked by her son, the famous Professor John Veitch of St Andrews and Glasgow, what the dwarf was really like, she replied: "There was a lot of good in the body, but he was gey ill-used."

May he rest in peace in Manor kirkyard. ▟

BIG SAM

J. L. Goskirk

In the porch of the manse which has been my home since 1969, there is a row of coat pegs six feet six inches above floor level. Some years ago, a visitor of no more than average height, reached up to hang his hat on one. "I don't know why these pegs are so high," I remarked, to which he replied, "Because the people of Sutherland were amongst the tallest in the country. After all," he went on, "Big Sam was a native of Lairg." Indeed Big Sam MacDonald was big enough to be mentioned under the heading "Tallest Scotsmen" in the *Guinness Book of Records*. This naturally intrigued me, and I set out to discover more about this amazing character.

Samuel MacDonald was born at Torroble in the Parish of Lairg in 1762. The Records go back only to 1768, so I was unable to find out the names of his parents, but they are said to have been no taller than average. Sam himself is said to have been a very delicate baby (possibly born prematurely), and his mother kept him by the fire on the big open hearth and fed him on nourishing mare's milk. What must have been their thoughts as their son grew far beyond the height of other lads, and how did they feed their growing lad adequately?

Sam's true height—full grown—is not easy to establish with any certainty. In the *Scotsman's Library* of 1825, and in local tradition, he is said to have been seven feet four inches, the *Guinness Book of Records* says six feet eight inches, while Michael Brander in his *Scottish Highlanders and their Regiments* has six feet ten inches, the height recorded on his tombstone. A difference of eight inches is considerable, but perhaps for those of merely average height, the most important thing was that Sam was fully 12 inches taller. All the sources are agreed that he was also built in proportion, his chest measurement being 48 inches. One writer says:—

> "Extremely strongly built and muscular, but yet proportional unless his legs might be thought even too big for the load they had to bear. His strength was prodigious, but such was his pacific disposition that he was never known to exert it improperly."

No doubt in his youth, Sam would have been in great demand for lifting and carrying loads beyond normal strength, and there is at least one house in Lairg with foundations going back 200 years with a massive corner stone said to have been laid by Sam. Much of his leisure time appears to have been spent putting the weight, and near the ruins of his home, the boulder he used for practising may still be seen.

In 1779, when Sam was 17, the 2nd Sutherland Fencibles were raised. Parish ministers were asked to provide lists of men between the ages of 16 and 60, and Sam must have been an obvious recruit. William Wemyss, son of the Hon. James

Wemyss and Lady Betty, was appointed Colonel and the regiment was assembled at Fort George.

For most of their existence, they were stationed in Edinburgh (Fencibles were raised for home service in time of war), but with the ending of the American War of Independence in 1783, they were disbanded, and Sam, then aged 21, enlisted in the 1st Foot (Royal Scots) and served for six years as a fugleman (a trained soldier who stands in front of a line of men and leads them by his movements in their drill). Obviously his great height made him particularly suitable for such a job, and it must have been during this time that he attracted the notice of the Prince of Wales (later King George IV) who employed him for about two years as a porter at his London mansion, Carlton House.

While in London, Sam appeared on the stage of the Opera House, Haymarket, in the role of Hercules in a classical play, "Cymon and Iphegenia", presented by the Drury Lane Company.

In 1792, the 3rd Sutherland Fencibles were raised, and Sam joined their ranks, being made a sergeant in the Colonel's company. When rebellion broke out in Ireland in 1797, the Fencibles were posted there, where it was recorded of them that, "their conduct and manners softened the horrors of war, and they were not a week in fresh quarters or cantonment that they did not conciliate and become intimate with the people."

Perhaps the fact that the men of Sutherland were native Gaelic speakers gave them a sympathy for the Irish and made them more acceptable. Many knew no English, and the Rev. Donald Sage in his *Memorabilia Domestica* records that, when the 93rd (Sutherland) Highlanders were raised in 1799, the Secretary of State sanctioned 4d. per day extra pay to four corporals to drill the men in Gaelic. On the suppression of the rebellion in Ireland, the regiment returned to Scotland and reduced at Fort George in 1798, but most of the men joined the 93rd, An Reismeid Cattach (the Sutherland Regiment) in the following year, along with their Colonel, Major General Wemyss of Wemyss. Sam was no exception. As the *Scotsman's Library* puts it "he could not be kept from his old friends, and joining the corps he remained with them until his death."

In the 93rd he was promoted to sergeant, and continued as supernumerary sergeant in the Colonel's company. He was considered excellent at drill on account of his mild and clear manner in giving directions. Sam was considered too large to be in the ranks and generally stood on the right. He had a pet—no doubt a kind of regimental mascot—"a mountain deer of uncommon size" which rarely left his side even when the regiment was on parade. When they were on the move, he and brother in arms, Sergeant MacKay, (six feet two inches) marched together with the hart accompanying them "to clear the road". No doubt the sight of the two giants heading the column was highly effective in achieving their aim.

Many anecdotes have been preserved which testify to Big Sam's great strength and sense of humour. When the 2nd Fencibles were stationed in Edinburgh, his enormous figure was, of course, a familiar sight, and one of the city's cab drivers used to torment him by flicking his whip. Sam was long-suffering, but eventually he had had enough and seized the cab from behind. So great was his strength that the horse was brought to a complete standstill and remained so until the cabbie apologised and Sam let them go.

It was, I understand, in Edinburgh Castle that he was posted as a sentry one

Big Sam MacDonald in the uniform of the Sutherland Fencibles (from *Kay's Biographical Sketches*).

night with only a dismounted gun to guard. After standing outside for some time, he marched into the guardroom with the gun over his shoulder, remarking that he could watch it just as well there as outside in the cold. Normally it would have taken three or four men to lift it.

On another occasion in barracks, one of his fellow soldiers asked Sam to hand down a loaf from a very high shelf. Sam's response was to grab him by the collar and lift him at arm's length with the words, "There, take it down yourself."

While stationed in Dublin, Sam was also conspicuous in his kilt and feathered bonnet, and was often the butt of less than good-natured teasing and banter. At that time, he was in charge of the regimental catering, and set off one day to buy meat from a butcher about two miles away. As they haggled over the price of a bullock, the butcher challenged Sam to carry it back to the barracks himself—if he succeeded he could have it for nothing! Sam hoisted the beast on to his broad shoulders and strode back leaving the butcher a wiser and sorrier man. The weight of an average bullock today might be in the region of 10 cwts, but even allowing for the smaller beasts of the times, Sam's burden was still probably around 7 cwts at least.

It was in Dublin, too, that Sam received an injury which may well have been responsible for his early death. A group of medical students, eager to examine his body naked, invited him to a local hostelry and after plying him liberally with drink until they considered he would be incapable of defending himself, they grabbed and attempted to strip him. Sam, however, was not so befuddled as they'd hoped, and soon cleared the room, throwing his assailants down the stairs. An angry crowd of Dubliners gathered in support of their compatriots and attacked Sam.

Before he was rescued, a blacksmith dealt him a blow on his head with his hammer which would have finished a lesser man, and almost certainly hastened his death four years later at the early age of 40.

At this period, the south of England was in constant fear of invasion by Napoleon, and in September 1800, the 93rd embarked for Guernsey in the Channel Islands. Sam died there and was buried in the Strangers' Cemetery in St. Peter Port on 9th May 1802. His burial place was marked by a tombstone erected by the non-commissioned officers of his regiment bearing the following inscription:

The
Body of

Serjeant SAMUEL MACDONALD

of the 93rd Regiment
or SUTHERLAND
HIGHLANDERS
was interred here on the
9th MAY
1802
Having served his King and Country
for 24 years
he died esteemed by his Officers
and beloved by his fellow Soldiers,
in the 41st Year of his age.
He measured when living,
six feet ten inches in height,
was well proportioned,
and of uncommon strength.
He was a native of the County of
Sutherland in Scotland.

In 1820, this inscription, which had become badly weathered, was renewed by the non-commissioned officers, and 50 years later, the monument, again in a bad state of repair, was restored by the officers of the regiment, on the initiative of Major Murchison, who had retired from the regiment and was living on the island.

The Strangers' Cemetery in St. Peter Port no longer exists, and it is not known what became of the memorial to Lairg's "gentle giant".

THE GREAT TOMMY MORGAN

Alex R. Mitchell gives his personal memories of the man he believes was the funniest Scots comic of them all.

The big, moon-faced man regarded by many as the greatest-ever exponent of West of Scotland humour died in November 1958. For close on thirty years I enjoyed the friendship of Tommy Morgan, the hoarse-voiced comedian from Bridgeton, Glasgow.

He packed the city's Pavilion Theatre every evening for 19 successive summers. In winter he played to big audiences in Edinburgh, Dundee and Belfast.

The many targets of his rough, astringent wit included councillors, snobs, football teams, misers . . . Glasgow folk of all classes. No one knew better the foibles and frailties of his fellow Glaswegians.

Morgan's comedy was broad, but never salacious. Unlike some of today's comedians, he never made jokes about people with physical disabilities. He was mortified once when a cross-eyed man confronted him outside the Pavilion and complained about a gag in the show.

By modern standards, it was innocuous enough. As Morgan told it, it went: "This wee fella had such a bad squint that no lassie would look at him. He was that depressed that he decided tae droon himself in the Clyde. He went doon tae Jamaica Bridge, climbed up on the parapet an jumped. But him bein sae squinty-eyed, he jumped the wrong way. Landed flat on his back on the pavement. 'Ma Goad!' he says, 'jist ma luck! The Clyde's frozen over in June!'"

Morgan apologised to the complainer and never told the joke again.

He was a fascinating man on and off stage, a man of many facets. He was a rough diamond, by turns aggressive and gentle, self-confident and insecure, cynical and sentimental. He was fond of recalling his humble beginnings—and in his case they were extremely humble.

Tommy Morgan, one of a large family, was born and brought up in a room and kitchen flat in one of Bridgeton's crumbling tenements in what he later called "Poverty Street." At the age of ten he rose at six o'clock each morning to deliver rolls.

"I managed to nick some for the family every day," he told me. "Ma mother was an honest wumman and thought this was a perk that went wi the job. But if it hudnae been for thae rolls, we'd have gone hungry many a time."

Morgan was 16 when the 1914–18 War started; overstating his age, he enlisted in the Army. On his 17th birthday he was under fire in a shell-hole in Flanders. He liked to relate the story of what happened when he set off from Glasgow after his first home leave. It was a typically Morganesque exploit.

The whole family went with him to Central Station to see him off on the London train. It was a tearful occasion and, as the train drew out of the station, the young soldier was overcome by a combination of fear of the future and homesickness.

A few minutes later the train made an unscheduled stop at Eglinton Street Station. Tommy at once pulled down the window in the locked door, threw out his kitbag and followed it out on to the platform. He trudged the four miles or so back

Tommy Morgan lays down the law to the chorus line at one of his successful Glasgow Pavilion shows.

PHOTO: GEORGE OUTRAM & COMPANY LTD

to Bridgeton and an old uncle let him into the house.

During this time the family were having a consolatory snack in a city centre cafe. When they got home they could hardly believe their eyes when they saw Tommy sitting at the fireside.

"I think they thought I was a ghost," he recalled. "Then ma faither realised that ghosts don't usually smoke fags and he glared at me. 'Whit the divvel are you daein here?' he yelled. Wi that he whipped off his bunnet and gave me the most awfy scud across the face. 'Get back tae the sojers!' he shouted. And back I went."

Private Morgan got through the war unscathed and, back in Civvy Street, went on the dole. He decided to emigrate to the States and with the help of the family managed to scrape up enough money for a one-way steamship ticket to New York. He did not have enough to buy himself an overcoat, and it was a particularly cold winter. Eventually he persuaded a friend to give him his after Morgan promised to send him £2 out of his first month's wages in New York.

However, he changed his mind about emigrating and renewed his efforts to find a job in Glasgow. One day he was standing at Bridgeton Cross wearing the overcoat when its rightful owner appeared. "So ye didnae emigrate!" he bellowed angrily. "Gie me back ma coat, ye swindler!" He thereupon ripped the overcoat from the back of the non-emigrant.

In the early 1920s Morgan teamed up with a friend, Tommy Yorke, to enter an amateur talent contest or "go-as-you-please competition," as it was called in those days. Yorke, a small, dark, mild-mannered man, was a would-be comedian and a frequent attender at the competitions. These were organised by small-time promoters in little halls and theatres.

Morgan was the feed or straight man in the new comedy partnership and the duo won top prize in their first contest. They went on to win many more in the year that followed.

Their first professional engagement was at a smoking concert. They were delighted with the fee—£2 between them. For ten years after that it was a hard slog for Yorke and Morgan round the small music halls then flourishing in Glasgow and the West.

It was a gruelling apprenticeship for the pair. Hecklers were plentiful and notoriously active on Friday nights, when they fortified themselves with strong drink against the rigours of watching fifth-rate entertainment while sitting on hard, wooden benches.

A painful memory for Morgan was that of his first appearance with his partner at the old Panoptican music hall in Argyle Street. He was puzzled when, in the vestibule before the show, he overheard the smiling doorman enquire of a patron, "Got your supplies all right, Wullie?"

"It turned out that the doorman was talkin aboot a big bag o bashed fruit and vegetables Wullie was carryin," Morgan explained. "It wasn't long before we learned it was the done thing for patrons to pelt the performers with all sorts of rubbish.

"I hudnae said two words on the stage before somebody in the audience shouted, 'Big bawface!' an a rotten tomato hit me smack between the eyes."

As the pair became better-known, the big aggressive Morgan became the comedian, the principal member of the partnership, and the act was billed as "Morgan and Yorke." The self-effacing smaller man was perfectly content to be the feed, a job he held for many years.

In the Thirties, Tommy Morgan's rise was rapid and his long series of summer shows at the Pavilion began. He was at his peak during the years of the last War which afforded him many subjects for his robust Glaswegian wit . . . the black-out, rationing, spivs, the Home Guard, Hitler, free-spending G. I.'s and romantically-inclined Polish soldiers. He delighted audiences with his character "Big Beenie," a larger-than-life Glasgow dame who figured in all sorts of earthy contretemps.

Morgan was devastated by the death of his wife, who had been of enormous help to him in his career, and for a time it was with difficulty that he carried on with his comedy at the Pavilion. Then several years after her death he married Celia Birmingham, the daughter of an old-time comedian.

Celia was also a great help to Morgan. Chic and charming, she knocked some of the rougher edges off her husband and made their home a very happy one.

Towards the end of the war, Morgan was in the big money, on a salary of several hundred pounds per week and also a percentage of the gross takings at the Pavilion. He revelled in his success and wealth. By now he was known as "Mr Glasgow". The title has been used by other comedians in the past few years, but to many middle-aged and elderly Glaswegians Tommy Morgan is still regarded as THE "Mr Glasgow".

By the end of the war, and in the ten years after it, he was cutting quite an expensive dash. His luxury flat in Great Western Road was extremely costly. His car, chauffeur-driven, was a big, long-bonneted Rolls-Bentley. His suits were made by one of the priciest tailors in Scotland. He drank sparingly, but the weekly drinks bill at the theatre came to over £20—his dressing-room at the Pavilion was always full of his friends.

He was perhaps unduly impressed by others who had succeeded in the entertainment world. The late Jack Hawkins was a particular hero and they became friends when they met in Majorca. He was a friend and admirer of the great actor and droll, Duncan Macrae. Stanley Baxter was a fan of Morgan and was always warmly welcomed in the Pavilion No. 1 dressing-room.

Tommy was delighted when the film star Cesar Romero called on him during rehearsals one forenoon. In his usual expansive way, Morgan announced that he was taking a party of us for lunch.

As we left the stage door in Renfield Street, Romero, a kindly, courteous man, was stopped by a wee stage-hand who had at one time worked in Hollywood. As they began to talk, Tommy walked on. However, the chat was lasting too long for Morgan, and when he reached Sauchiehall Street he turned and shouted, "Come oan, Cesar! We're gaun doon for wur dinner!"

Some of the frugality of his early days remained with him and this was demonstrated after he asked me where he could find someone who could write music for him—an opening chorus for his summer show and other bits and pieces.

I recommended a friend, Jimmy Gilbert, a young actor-composer. Arrangements were made, and Gilbert wrote some excellent music. Morgan was delighted with it . . . but he wasn't so pleased when the composer sent in his bill—£66. He paid up, but complained to me, "I gied him mair notes than he gied me!"

Monte Landis and two friends were doing a highly-successful comedy routine in one of the Pavilion summer shows. Monte thought that he and his colleagues deserved a pay rise. "You're doing all right," he pointed out to Morgan. "Can you pay us a little more?"

Morgan gave him a cold, blue-eyed stare, then, with concentrated ferocity, he barked two words—"You're oot!" And out of the show went the trio, each with the requisite two weeks' salary in lieu of notice.

To his Pavilion company Morgan was known as "The Guv'nor." He put on the show himself and paid the artistes out of earnings. His word was law. When he rehearsed a sketch, he never uttered the lines he was to say, but the supporting players had to jot down their lines at Morgan's dictation. He told them when they had to enter and exit.

When the sketch was performed before an audience the supporting cast heard his gags for the first time and often they were hard put to keep from laughing. A bleak stare from The Guv'nor made them quickly control their mirth.

Gruff and ruthless though he sometimes was, Morgan was also a kindly man. Many a theatrical down on his or her luck received a weekly retainer from him. In a trouser pocket he carried a wad of notes, and he was always ready to peel one or two off it to

The Pavilion Theatre, Glasgow, scene of many of Tommy Morgan's great performances.

give to anyone who "tapped" him.

He was ever a creature of impulse. One day he suddenly decided to visit his childhood haunts in Bridgeton. Two old women recognised him and one said, "Aw, Tommy, Ah wish Ah had a photie o ye!" He at once sent for a photographer. "The three o us will get taken thegither, hen," he told her.

It turned out to be a good, clear picture, but alas, it was spoiled by the background. On the wall just above the heads of the trio was a large printed inscription—a most bigoted and scurrilous reference to a well-known religious leader. Tommy paid a second visit to Bridgeton and the photograph was retaken.

Another impulse came to him when he was crossing France on his way to Nice in his Rolls-Bentley. The chauffeur must have bitterly regretted switching on the radio. From it came the excited voice of a football commentator. Morgan listened for a few seconds. Then—"Here, I forgot! Celtic's playin Rangers next Saturday! Turn the car roon! We're gaun back hame!" And back home they went.

Alec Finlay, that other great comic, told me of an impulse that struck Morgan when they met on holiday in Majorca. He suddenly decided to take a party to a favourite night-club in Barcelona.

"Right away he chartered a plane", said Alec. "Off we all flew to Barcelona, visited the night-club and got back to Majorca at dawn the next day. He insisted on paying for everything. 'Ma wee treat,' he said."

In the late Fifties the good times were coming to an end for Tommy Morgan . . . to be succeeded by tragedy and mystery.

He began to suffer from blinding headaches, but, in the old, show-must-go-on tradition, he continued in his summer season at the Pavilion. Eventually, almost worn out by pain, he agreed to consult a specialist . . . and the blow fell. Morgan was found to be suffering from a brain tumour and an immediate operation was deemed necessary.

It was a success and I visited him often when he was convalescing at his home. His fine, dark hair had been shaved off and he had lost weight. Nevertheless he was still, as he put it, "comin awa wi a gag." One afternoon he said, "I've some photies tae show ye." I wondered what to expect.

They were large X-ray photographs of his head, rather off-putting to me, but Tommy was delighted with them and proud of the fact that the operation had been such a difficult one.

"I'd rather be one of these great surgeons than the biggest star in the world," he said wistfully. Then he added, "Mind ye, if I'd known the inside o ma heid was like that, I'd never have had the nerve to walk on a stage."

His hair was short and white when he went back to the Pavilion for a season. His fans flocked to see him and he was greatly heartened by their loyalty. It was a desperate struggle, though, and only he would know fully the mental and physical agony he endured as, in his usual way, he worked hard to raise laughs.

As that season came to an end he lost the power of his right leg and there had to be another operation. It, too, was successful and he announced his intention of going back to work.

Sad to say, he had become very frail. His tragic battle ended on a foggy day in November 1958, when, at the age of 60, he died peacefully in his flat.

He left a mystery behind him. The hard-working comedian who for many years had earned several hundred pounds a week, died practically penniless. Some said that he had gambled secretly, others that he was extravagant and too generous with his hospitality and his handouts to needy friends and acquaintances. The mystery has never been solved.

Hundreds of Glasgow folk who had laughed at and with him over many years attended his funeral. They sensed correctly that they would never see his like again.

I remember big, bluff Tommy Morgan with great affection. He certainly brought a great measure of fun into my life. ▐

WHAT THEY READ THEN

The intended demolition of the cross of Edinburgh has now taken place. As soon as the workmen began, which was in the morning of March 13, some gentlemen who had spent the night over a social bottle, caused wine and glasses be carried thither, mounted the ancient fabric, and solemnly drank its dirge. The beautiful pillar which stood in the middle, fell, and broke to pieces, by one of the pullies used on that occasion, giving way. It was one stone, about twenty feet high and eighteen inches diameter, of an octagon figure, and finely spangled with gilded thistles, etc. After passing the act of sederunt of the court of session (33.), the court of justiciary, Jan. 21. approved likewise of this alteration.

On Saturday, March 20, about two o'clock after noon, some gentlemen walking in the south garden of the abbey of Holyrood-house, belonging to George Fyfe, were surprised by a great noise, like the rattling of many coaches. It was occasioned by a most extraordinary whirlwind, which continued above a minute, raising every moveable from the ground and agitating in a violent manner some linen that were on a hedge. A course apron, tore off the hedge, was carried up with surprising velocity, till it appeared no larger than a common crow, continued waving in the air more than a quarter of an hour, and at last fell slowly from a prodigious height upon some part of Arthur's seat.

There was a perfect calm before and after; and the gentlemen declare they felt not the least wind even at the time, though they were within forty yards of the circle of the whirlwind.

From *The Scots Magazine,* March 1756.

WHAT THEY READ THEN

The freshest intelligence from Scotland mentions the arrival of four ships in all in the North ports of that kingdom, with arms, etc. for the use of the rebels, viz. one at Montrose, two at Stonehaven, and the fourth at Dunnotyr; that the cargo of the first was carried South in 85 carts, and that of two others, in more than a hundred, drawn each by two horses; that they brought some brass cannon, and one piece of five inches bore, with some gunners and officers; that 1000 recruits, mostly Atholmen, joined the rebels at Dalkeith on the 31st past; as did, late the same night, 400 men from Alloa, (where they had secured a passage over the Forth), who brought with them six pieces of brass cannon; that they had with them above 100 carts, loaded partly with chests, and partly with biscuit, and twelve or sixteen French engineers; that the Pretender's son, attended by those called the life-guards, left Edinburgh at six that evening, and lodged at Pinkie, four miles East of the city; that next day he proceeded to Dalkeith, whence two bodies of Highlanders marched in the evening of Pennycuik and Loanhead, two places at a small distance on the road leading to Peebles, Moffat, Carlisle, etc; that the whole army was to follow next day, the Pretender's son to set out from Dalkeith 3d, and to march through Annandale to Carlisle; that, the better to disguise their motions, billets for quarters had been sent to Mussel-burgh, Fisher-row, Inveresk, Prestonpans, Tranent, Haddington, and other villages upon the East-road to Berwick, whilst considerable numbers were to march by night to the Westward; that they had along with them above 150 carts and waggons full of baggage, besides great numbers of baggage-horses; and that they gave out, that their intention was, to proceed directly into England, to slip Marshal Wade, and to get into Lancashire.

About the end of September, the King ordered a strong body of troops, consisting of several battalions of foot and some squadrons of horse and dragoons, to march directly to Scotland, under the command of Field-Marshal Wade. They were appointed to assemble at Doncaster, for which place the Marshal set out from London on the 6th of October. His Excellency and the army were at Doncaster on the 19th, at Darlington on the 26th, and at Newcastle on the 29th; whence it was proposed to march on towards Edinburgh in a day or two thereafter. – Lt-Gen. Handasyd arrived at Berwick about the 19th, and took upon him the command of the forces there.

A Royal proclamation was issued, of date Oct. 5. promising every able-bodied man who shall inlist for the land-service on or before the 25th of December next, that he shall, upon his request, be discharged at the end of six months, or when the present rebellion shall be extinguished.

From *The Scots Magazine*, October 1745.

OUT AND ABOUT

NIGHT ON BIRD ISLAND

Rennie McOwan

It's like Hell," said a sleepy voice. So it was for an hour or two. It was like one of those engravings from books of the 1800s showing the perils of mountain and sea to would-be travellers, or an old illustration for a tale of damnation.

The Victorians especially went in for that kind of thing. Chasms yawned, beetling precipices frowned, huge waves never before seen on earth dwarfed fragile ships. Everything looked black, threatening, slightly macabre and not a little frightening.

My view was not all that different. It was late evening and my companion Bobby Peat and I were lying in sleeping-bags in a little hollow near the end of the island-breakwater of Dun which forms one side of Village Bay on the island of Hirta in the St Kilda group. It was a dry night, but to our left and behind us, over the edge of the nose of the island, we could hear the ceaseless booming of the sea.

Our hollow was surrounded by large boulders and rocks, piled crazily on top of one another. They smelled of fish, and from their dark recesses came a constant noise of movements, rustlings and scrapings, squeaks and little cries as the shags, fulmars, guillemots and razorbills stirred in sleep or moved around. To our left, towering seawards, and overlooking us, were the huge cliffs of the highest part of Dun, seamed and wrinkled and cut by years of wind and storm.

The darkening sky was criss-crossed by the shapes of hundreds of birds—kittiwakes, razorbills and puffins. There was an endless soaring and wheeling, turning the sky into a continual pattern of movement.

The blackness, the high cliffs and shadowy rocks, the smell, the constant cries and the crash of the sea, together produced an atmosphere of a different world. This may sound fanciful, but that is what it was like. It is a different world. Dun (pronounced Doon) is a world which, compared with many islands, and even with the main St Kildan island of Hirta, does not receive many human visitors. It is cut off from Hirta by a channel through which the sea surges at high tide.

Dun can be reached by boat only when the sea is calm, and visitors have to leap ashore over wet and slippery rocks, with a precarious scramble up the shore ahead of them.

It is possible to cross the Dun Gap, as it is known, by waiting for a calm sea and low tide. A wet and delicate way can sometimes be picked across submerged boulders avoiding the deep pools either side. The cliffs ahead then have to be scaled.

We crossed to Dun by breeches-buoy which research naturalists had rigged up across the Gap. It has since been removed.

Nothing molests the birds here. There is little or no animal life—no rabbits, weasels,

The fulmar was once found only on St Kilda but now breeds throughout the British Isles. Watching the bird's gliding flight was an absorbing activity when Rennie McOwan was on Dun.

PHOTO: TOM WEIR

stoats, foxes or sheep. The birds treat a human visitor as a harmless curiosity. A few feet from where we lay, a row of guillemots, razorbills and a few shags lined the cliff. If we moved, they would do a sideways shuffle, and perhaps take off for a few lazy strokes before landing again, but no more than that.

It is another world—a world where man is a stranger.

We had been on St Kilda for almost a fortnight, as members of the National Trust for Scotland's last working party of the summer, helping to repair and maintain the old school and church, and carrying out other work. The working parties are part of the continuing story of St Kilda—this tiny archipelago 45 miles west of the Outer Hebrides—whose population was finally evacuated in 1930, ending their unique and lonely way of life.

The National Trust for Scotland now owns the islands and leases them to the Nature Conservancy Council which has designated them a National Nature Reserve. They are of great importance to naturalists. St Kilda is Britain's most important seabird breeding location—it has the largest gannetry in the world and the oldest colony of fulmars in Britain.

Each summer, the Trust organises parties which restore the ancient cottages and cleits and enjoy themselves into the bargain. A party is limited to 12, including a leader, and each person agrees to work for part of every day.

Our fortnight also included talks on the geology and history of the island and splendid walks and exploration around the towering cliffs, the highest in Britain. We saw the splendour of the tunnel-cavern and watched the seals sporting in the waves. We visited the smooth grass of the Cambir with its dramatic views of the stacs and the sheep island of Soay, and Gleann Mor with the remains of ancient settlements and its legend of an Amazon queen.

We had listened to the constant "drumming" of the snipe, got irritated by the oystercatchers' piercing whistles as they became anxious about their chicks, and dodged the aerial attacks of the skuas as we approached their nests. We ate huge meals and slept the sleep of the exhausted.

Nevertheless the highlight for Bobby Peat and me was the visit to Dun.

It was our second-last night. The research naturalists had planned to cross to Dun, on the breeches-buoy, to ring puffins. They said two others could also go, and Bobby and I volunteered.

With the help of two soldiers from the Army's small tracking station in Village Bay, we hauled on the ropes and sent one another spinning across the void to the rocks on the far side. The rucksacks followed. The naturalists quickly unloaded their gear and settled down for a night of ringing and weighing puffins.

Our base was at the far end of the island so, shoulders bowed, we said good-bye to them and left the edge of the rocks to begin our walk.

The contrast between Hirta and Dun was startling. On one side of the channel was an island with the grass cropped short by sheep.

On the other, the vegetation was untouched, lush, green and knee-high. There were many flowers. Other than the tracks of the naturalists on previous visits, it was unbroken by human feet. The earth smelled strongly. It was like the edge of a Lowland wood in mid-summer. The only things missing, happily, were flies and midges. With a sea breeze blowing almost continually, and very little standing water, St Kilda is largely free of these pests. We ploughed on through the vegetation, trying to follow the crest of the long Dun ridge.

Walking became difficult because the ground is tunnelled by a labyrinth of puffins' burrows until the earth becomes undermined. Care was needed in case a whole section turned over under our feet to send us crashing down the steep slope.

Puffins were everywhere. They perched on every rock, circled overhead, flew to

Guillemots above and razorbills below. Rennie McOwan observed them from only a few feet away.   PHOTO: TOM WEIR

and fro, shot out of burrows, or waddled inside as we approached. One flew out of a burrow at my feet and its spreadeagled, squat legs caught the top of the grasses bowling it head-over-heels. They were certainly living up to their name of sea-clowns. Their perky size, bright eyes, multicoloured beaks and general gait are an endearing sight.

Our progress was slow. The steep ground, the thick plants and the insecure footing made us take great care.

We halted a couple of times, admiring the effortless curving glides of the fulmars, the kittiwakes, and farther out, the gannets.

From holes in the rocks came the angry squeaking of young fulmars, and we took care passing these holes as the young spat a foul-smelling oil at us whenever they got a clear view.

We began to clamber over large blocks of rock, searching for a place to spend the night.

It looked as if we might have accidentally passed the best place. However, when we were about three-quarters of the way along Dun, and had crossed the highest point, we found a wide shelf surrounded by blocks of

The gannet breeds in large numbers on the St Kilda islands. 　　　　PHOTO: TOM WEIR

rocks and thick with vegetation. It was saucer-shaped, and the slight hollow gave us a feeling of security with the cliff edge on either side being only a few yards away. We dumped our rucksacks, and with the weight off our backs scrambled quickly over the slabs until we were at the very end of Dun and could see the sea creaming on the rocks.

The sky began to grow dark, so we returned to our saucer, spread out ground-sheets and sleeping-bags and settled down for the night. The vegetation was so thick that it felt like an air mattress.

We talked comfortably, watching the aerial parade overhead and basking in the atmosphere of this unique and lonely place.

Late at night, I half-awoke to hear

[97]

G

Bobby's urgent voice. The air seemed full of an odd whistling and the swish of wings.

The night flight of the shearwaters and petrels had begun, the birds heading unerringly through the darkness for the holes and crevices in the rocks. The night became alive with movement. A constant and eerie "churring" and piping came out of the darkness, and we listened drowsily, but intrigued by the manoeuvres of these fascinating birds which stay out at sea during the day and head for their underground refuges at night.

It was difficult to identify the dark bodies, but experts say the night fliers would be made up of Manx shearwaters, the bat-like storm petrel and the rarer Leach's petrel.

In the morning, the black cliffs were transformed. A bright sun touched the tops with yellow and pink and everything sparkled.

We emptied the vacuum flasks and ate our remaining sandwiches.

We had a final orgy of exploration, closely examining a dressed stone wall, skilfully built above the cliffs at the end of Dun. It is said to have been a fort and to have given its name to the island, but some St Kilda travellers disagree and say that it is an ancient barrier to prevent sheep or cattle tumbling into the sea. They claim that the name Dun is a corruption of the Gaelic word donn (brown).

The wall is certainly a puzzle and so are the regular lines of what in certain lights look like "cultivation terraces" near the Dun Gap.

We began the long walk back to the channel and the breeches-buoy and Bobby made an energetic diversion to the highest point. We crossed without incident other than my arms running out of strength when Bobby was three-quarters way over. A bout of heaving and tugging eventually landed him on the other side.

I followed on, and we both got an overhead view of some eider ducks cruising alongside the rocks.

We returned to our cottage at 5 a.m., demolished a gigantic breakfast and fell asleep.

At midday we all received an urgent summons. Bad weather was imminent and our boat would call for us the next day, 24 hours earlier than planned.

Sleep was abandoned, and a frenzy of packing begun.

We had snatched a unique night just in time. ◨

TAKING THE MUNROS BY STORM

Martin Moran recalls impressions of the fastest-ever continuous ascent of all our 3000 foot-plus mountains in the freezing weather of winter 1984/85.

An idea as ambitious as climbing all 277 Munros in a single winter requires ample justification. Many would doubt the sanity of someone who sets out to attain an average of three summits over 3000 feet on each of 90 consecutive days, through the darkness, storms and snows of our most cruel season. After all, who in their right mind would head off with boundless enthusiasm into the frozen wilderness in late December at a time when most people are content to warm their toes by Christmas fires?

Even hillgoers might scorn the escapade as a pointless and dangerous test of endurance, courting hardship and hazard for their own sakes, and treating the mountains as a glorified racetrack.

Such reactions were only to be expected when I broached my intention to attempt this very feat. It was a radical undertaking, far removed from climbing traditions—a venture never previously tried, and perhaps never even contemplated. The essential question "Why?" demands an answer at the outset.

I have a deep and long-held passion for mountains, especially those of Scotland. No dedicated climbers can consider their love requited unless they have sampled the hills in all seasons, and I harboured a great fascination to explore the qualities unique to winter.

However worthy my aspirations, they required a long apprenticeship in the Alps and Himalaya as well as this country, and more immediately a period of detailed and methodical planning in order to give a reasonable chance of success.

The complete collection of Highland Ordnance Survey maps was my nightly companion for many months as I schemed and plotted the most efficient routes. I produced a schedule taking 80 days averaging 14 miles, and 5500 feet of ascent with a 10-day allowance for sitting out the worst storms.

Against this, I pitched the likely weather patterns that I would face, for I had researched the meteorological data for recent years. With an anticipated 40 days of gale-force winds at 3000 feet, I concluded that the venture lay on the borders of possibility, as dependent on the vagaries of the weather as it was on my personal skills and endurance.

Clearly, I needed to apply tactics to reduce the unfavourable odds. Firstly, my wife Joy joined me to provide company and support throughout the trip. What an emotional boost it was to have her help when my spirits fell to a low ebb! Then we hired a motor caravan to provide transport and comfortable and convenient accommodation.

Although three people have achieved continuous self-propelled journeys over the Munros in spring and summer—Hamish Brown was the first in 1974—all have taken substantially longer than 90 days. Furthermore, the winter ascent would be a mountaineering proposition of an altogether more difficult and serious nature. Therefore it was essential to use a vehicle to move between the mountains if I was to hold any hope of completing them within the season.

The journey demanded no small personal sacrifice from us both. We resigned our jobs, and sold our Sheffield home in order to provide the necessary time and finance. The chilling sensation that we had pulled the rug from under our feet assailed us relentlessly as the starting date approached.

The pressure was increased by our decision to do the climbs in aid of the charity, Intermediate Technology, which works to alleviate rural poverty in the developing world. In the interests of promoting and raising funds for this worthy cause, we were exposed to a wave of media attention even before we began. We found ourselves irreversibly committed to the venture both personally and publicly.

Perhaps understandably, relief was my predominant feeling when we took the starting steps up the first Munro, Ben Lomond. As we were swallowed up in the summit clouds, all doubts and worries dissolved, for Nature's raw simplicity immediately banished our worldly cares. We had that delicious sense of freedom which always accompanies any excursion into the hills; but with three months stretching ahead, we felt more permanently absorbed into a wonderful new existence.

Emerging from the mists on the descent, we saw the rooftops of houses and factories in Dumbarton glistening in the low sunlight. Down there, people continued their daily round—many working, others celebrating the coming Christmas break; but few able to envisage the magical world we had entered just a few miles away.

At the end of the same day, my mood had reversed. We had reached the summit of Beinn Buidhe above Loch Fyne just as nightfall eclipsed a miserable afternoon of mist and sleet. Stumbling down the snowy slopes by torchlight, I was exhausted and depressed. Just 275 mountains left to climb, the whole fury of winter's storms yet to be unleashed, and more immediately the prospect of the next morning's 6 a.m. reveille—had I stepped on an unending treadmill?

Happily I never felt that way again. There was too much to see and appreciate. The constantly changing texture of mountains and weather as well as the succession of personal events and encounters ensured that each day bore its own individual stamp.

The target of 90 days forced me to engage the hills in all but the most severe weather. I often forsook the comforts of the glen only to be given a real drubbing on the tops. Yet these same days, when the peaks resounded to the blast of a tempest, also provided great exhilaration and drama.

The great switchback of the Mamores Ridge gave a particularly memorable tussle. I found myself atop the first summit, Mullach nan Coirean, on a wild gusty morning when no casual climber would have stayed to endure the buffeting.

On the ninth Munro, Binnein Mor, my strength and time were exhausted and I descended to Kinlochleven, leaving the remaining two—Binnein Beag and Sgurr Eilde Mor for another day. Although I failed in the complete traverse, that day was truly stolen out of the fire and one of the most exciting. It transpired that the outstanding pair were my final peaks just 41 days later.

Scotland's winter weather is infinitely varied, and wholly unpredictable. Rapid deteriorations can trap the unwary in deadly blizzards, but against this are the clearances which are just as sudden and even more surprising. After unending days of storm, you can awake to a world transformed—crystal clear, and not a

Martin and Joy on the slopes of Carn Liath in the Creag Meagaidh range. On days like this the great expedition became sheer delight.   PHOTO: HAMISH M. BROWN

breath of wind; the mountains iced with hoar and rime, and calling irresistibly.

At Cluanie Inn we waited tensely in such a storm. The prospect of four days on the remote Glen Affric hills was hardly inviting. As late as 6 a.m. on the morning of our intended departure, the squalls were rocking the caravanette like a baby's cradle. Yet two hours later, we strode onto Sgurr na Conbhairean in no more than a fresh breeze, and with the hills dappled in soft sunlight.

The ever-changing mantle of snow and ice can alter the appearance of peaks from day to day and play havoc with climbing conditions. Overnight the Black Cuillin of Skye can become the sugar-coated peaks of fairyland—as I found to my cost! The anticipated romp on dry rock was unexpectedly transformed into a nightmarish crawl along a treacherous crocodile of fresh wet snow, with the ice-caked Inaccessible Pinnacle as the terrifying climax.

Hills are more sharply distinguished in winter; the sandstone turrets of the Northwest take on an Alpine splendour while the

Cairngorm plateaux become as barren as the Arctic.

I find the snow infinitely preferable to the drenching rain of other seasons. Indeed, the times when I felt closest to suffering exposure were when I was soaked through in dreich conditions rather than in the fierce but dry blizzards.

For three weeks in January, I made speedy progress over iron-hard ground gripped in Siberian frosts. No mire impeded my progress or frayed my temper. In this period, the main obstacle was the sheet ice on all the tracks and along the glen roads. Once above this, life was easy!

In the ice-bound weeks of mid-February, I found the high Cairngorms swept to an even surface of névé snow. Hardened and burnished by the daily cycle of sun and frost, it was a joy to walk on and progress was considerably faster than in summer.

When the snow is really deep, you can always put on skis, but, alas, I chose the least snowy winter of the last decade for my expedition. I managed a paltry total of six days on skis, but these included a marvellous trip across the wide expanses of the Monadhliath from Newtonmore to Glen Shirra. As I sped over the four Munros there, a vast expanse of the Highlands was laid out on the horizon—from Ben Wyvis in the north to the Shiel hills on the west, Ben Lawers in the south and the Grampian massif stretching east. It was here I felt truly in the centre of the country.

The 21 miles flashed by in a mere seven hours which in retrospect were all too short, but, at the day's end when legs are tired, the final descent to the glen can be the last straw, especially on the skinny cross-country skis. I certainly left no pleasing patterns on the slopes, more the effect of a detonated minefield!

Solitude and loneliness characterise winter travels almost everywhere in the Highlands except the popular climbing areas of Ben Nevis and Glencoe. Utter silence reigns supreme and although this can frighten the unprepared, it gives me inspiration.

The mountain landscape acquires a timeless quality. Ugly modern scars made by eroded paths, dammed lochs and bulldozed tracks, so painfully apparent in summer, are happily lost under the snows. You can be transported to the era of your choice and live out the dream for a brief few hours.

Because of the absence of sounds, you are more aware of the few that are encountered, particularly those made by wildlife. Mountain creatures provide great interest in winter by their scarcity, and only the repetitive croak of the ptarmigan ever became tiresome.

Deer movements were especially fascinating. The herds seemed to sense the imminent passage of bad weather, and congregated in sheltered glen hollows. Many mornings, I climbed past the countless imprints of their overnight couches on the lower slopes, but of course the herd was already up and on the move however early my start.

On two occasions, in Glen Shiel and Glen Tilt, I heard gunshots ringing out as the winter cull of hinds took place. I assumed the stalkers would have an easy job with the herds seeking forage in the glens. They hardly needed to walk more than a few yards from their vehicles to find prey. However, I later learned that the winter cull can be more difficult. The animals sense the presence of humans much more keenly on snow-covered ground where there are no conflicting scents to confuse them.

I felt like a modern St Francis whenever I passed sheep in the glens. Thinking me to be the shepherd, they would crowd around ready for their feed. When sturdy farm horses got the same idea, I didn't hang about!

Although mountaineers are assured of solitude on winter hills, it is inevitable that they seek company—both to share the joys of the experience and to provide vital support in the event of mishap. Joy climbed 120 of the Munros with me, but on some days when I had to leave her, I felt an aching loneliness. This was never more acute than at the Corrour Bothy when I set out for a two-day trek over the Macdhui plateau in a milky white-out. Endless hours of tense navigation lay ahead without so much as a chink of view to rouse my spirits.

Companionship is more deeply appreciated in winter. Similarly, every meeting with other hillgoers takes on a greater significance. I remember deviating nearly a quarter of a mile on Beinn a' Bhuird to meet and chat to a lone ski-tourer. He probably felt a similar pleasure in this spirit of camaraderie (at least I hope so) which highlighted an otherwise lonely day.

Winter is the great time of year for bothying. Gathering in a Highland howff provides the ideal antidote to the overpowering loneliness of the hills. My bothy nights in Knoydart in mid-January provide my own fondest reflections. Coming off Sgurr na Ciche into the evening darkness after a 20-mile slog from Quoich Dam, I was desperate to locate the tiny Sourlies Bothy on the shore of Loch Nevis. I craved a roof over my head, and arrived in an intensely anti-social mood thinking solely of my own needs and woes. Expecting to find an empty refuge, I couldn't believe my ears when I heard the chatter of Geordie accents. Taken aback at first, I very quickly unwound and was amazed to discover two married bank managers on a week's trek in these deserted glens.

The following afternoon I arrived at Barrisdale Bothy in a state of exhaustion. I had crossed Meall Buidhe and Luinne Bheinn at a snail's pace, eaten the last of my food, and for the first time really doubted my ability to continue the expedition. To my great relief, Joy had already arrived. A roaring fire was warming the inner bedroom, soup was bubbling on the cooker and there were fresh vegetables, eggs and fruit to follow. In a couple of hours I had forgotten the hostile cold outside, and was even looking forward to the next day's ascent of Ladhar Bheinn. Such are the delights of winter bothying, and even if you do get a night to yourself there are always the mice for company!

We valued every contact that we made with local people. Several times we needed assistance when our vehicle met a snowdrift, and a willing pair of hands was usually close by.

It was most heart-warming to receive the good wishes and support of people in shops and garages. Nearly everyone had knowledge of my exploits from the papers or radio, and although many may have seen little sense in what I was doing, we never heard a dissenting voice.

Many times my identity was laid bare with pinpoint accuracy by perceptive Highlanders. When I arrived at Fealar Lodge by the headwaters of the Tilt in pitch darkness, I was chilled with fear to see ghostly lights. Approaching with real trepidation, I was stunned to be greeted by the friendly voice of Jimmy Lean the shepherd. His wife Dorothy already had the kettle boiled, having seen the flicker of my torch on Carn Bhac.

As I stepped into the light of their cottage (Scotland's highest permanently occupied farm as I later discovered), his eyes gleamed with recognition: "You'll be the chap who's doing all the Munros this winter!"

After more than an hour of animated talk,

277 down and none to go! The end of the 83-day non-stop ascent of all our summits over 3,000 feet took place on Sgurr Eilde Mor in the Mamores. Joy was with Mike in both senses of the word.

PHOTO: ALAN THOMSON

my drooping eyelids forced me to seek rest. Instead of the expected bivouac in an open sheep fank, I was shown to a comfortable bed, feeling a most distinguished guest.

As much as anything, a winter in Scotland's mountains has left me with a lasting respect. Joy and I will never forget the experience of setting off a massive avalanche on Ben Wyvis when we stepped over the edge of its summit cornice in a white-out. This was the one occasion when I went beyond the limits of experience. However, disasters require only one error and many climbers are not granted a second chance. Even the easier hills, such as Wyvis, demand a cautious and humble approach.

It is no exaggeration that winter's fury can make conditions on the Munros as serious as any in the world. The severe wind-chill I experienced on the Cairngorm plateau at $-35°C$ equalled anything I met on the 20,000 ft. Mount McKinley in Alaska. On eastern hills such as the Cairngorms, climbers must be alert to south-easterly winds. Any predicted windspeed should be doubled to allow for the jet-foil effect of the gentle plateau slopes. In gusts of over 90 mph, I was forced to crawl on hands and knees, clinging desperately to my ice axe for support.

On 13th March, 83 days after the first steps on Ben Lomond, we strode onto Sgurr Eilde Mor to claim our final Munro. Behind, lay over 1000 miles of hillwalking and 412,000 feet of ascent, but no collection of statistics can express the emotional depth of the experience.

North to the deserted straths of Sutherland, west to the Cuillin of Skye and east over the Grampian wastes—we had struggled against the storms, and fought the threat of exhaustion. Instead of immediate elation, we felt only sadness that our intimate acquaintance with these magnificent mountains was now at an end. A lasting satisfaction came at a later stage and particularly when we saw that our appeal had raised over £15,000.

What of the future? Many friends thought that after a winter of intensive Munro-bagging I would have been satisfied. The effect is quite the opposite. The expedition served to nurture my love for the Highlands into fuller blossom.

We are now living in Torridon, in our opinion the finest of all mountain areas, where, as a guide, I hope to introduce others to the special joys of winter climbing.

With my ardour undiminished, I watch the seasons turn, and look forward to the onset of other winters. A repeat of the Munro venture might be too much to contemplate, but whether it is ice-climbing, ski-ing or gentle exploring, I hope to be there. ▮

REMOTEST NORTH

Thomas Weir

This was the first article in *The Scots Magazine* by the man who was to become its longest-serving regular contributor with the start of the widely-read "My Month" series in 1956. "Thomas", of course soon became "Tom".

A walking-cum-climbing holiday in north-west Sutherland is not planned overnight—at least not by those who wish to eat at fairly regular intervals. Deciding where we would go was the simplest of our problems.

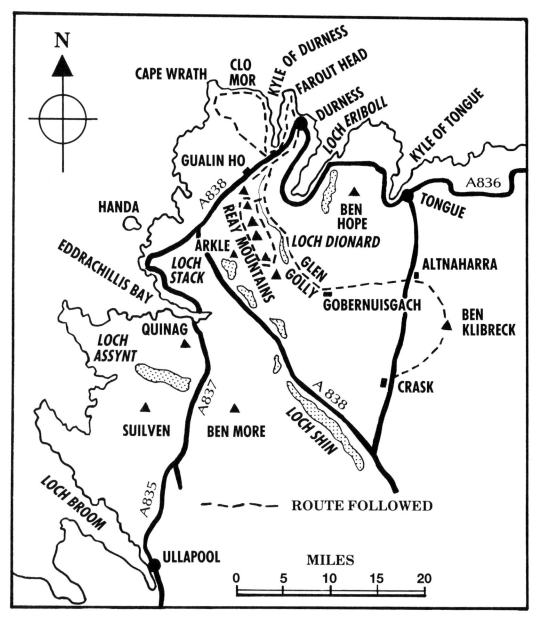

Map showing the route taken in north-west Sutherland by Tom Weir on his first expedition to be recorded in *The Scots Magazine*.

We would cross over Ben Klibreck, and then go via Strath Mor and Glen Golly to Strath Dionard, explore the peaks of the Reay Forest, and finish up at Clo Mor for some bird-watching at the biggest cliffs on the British mainland. Geese were supposed to nest on the moors somewhere, and snow buntings were reputed to nest on the tops. There was the chance, too, of seeing the pine marten on its home ground, for this sparsely inhabited country which stretches to Cape Wrath is said to be its real stronghold in Scotland.

To accomplish this, some staff work was necessary. We wanted to be self-supporting yet carry the bare minimum of equipment. Some letter writing followed and we received the generous offer of a bothy in the wilds of Strath Dionard, and another at Gobernuisgach, handy for Glen Golly. This would save us carrying tents for the first part of the trip. A depot for tents and surplus stores was fixed at Gualin House— all our arrangements were now complete.

The day was cloudy and the chill round our ears was certainly not imagination as we loaded our kit aboard the train. The newspapers that day forecast sleet and snow on the high ground and, sure enough, at Drumochter the hail was beating against the windows and the clouds advancing to meet us were unmistakably snow-laden.

It is a slow journey from Inverness to Lairg, with long halts at each stop, and a leisurely wait at this terminus while mail is sorted. However, it gave us a chance to do some shopping and divide our gear into six loads, three of which went on the Durness car, while we and the other three lots went on the Tongue bus.

Crask was our destination for a crossing of Ben Klibreck, but the scene was far from reassuring. Clouds trailed on the moors and hail beat from time to time on the windows of our bus. Klibreck itself thrust a snowy shoulder into a mass of black cloud, boding ill for our plan. However, after the inactivity of the long journey, we were glad to get out, hail or not, and following a fine path we took to the hill at a furious pace.

The climb was up a long, peaty shoulder. On the summit-ridge, things were more interesting. A blink of sun cleared the top of mist and lit most spectacularly a towering bank of cumulus that stood above the vastness of inky moors and trailing vapours. The snow was deep for a May fall, five inches to a foot being met with for the last 600 feet. All too soon we were enveloped in a blizzard.

From the summit we plunged steeply to the little inn at Altnaharra, where our rucksacks awaited us. The staff work was paying its dividends, for not only was a car provided to take us to Gobernuisgach, but a hot dinner was also laid on.

It was dusk and the landscape looked empty and dreary, as only Sutherland can, as we bumped our way to Strath Mor to reach the oasis of Gobernuisgach at the entrance to Glen Golly. The keeper was as good as his word, and soon we were lodged in the wash-house, with our wet clothes steaming in front of a peat fire, while we lay snug in our sleeping-bags on the floor.

Sunshine streaming in through the window roused us, though it was only 6.30 a.m. Outside, the ground was hard with frost, and Ben Hope glistened in crinkled snow high above the shadowy strath. Every little pocket was revealed in the slanting sunlight. Towards the Reay Forest the peaks were filmy with morning mist hanging on their quartz crests. A thread of blue and gold edged with brilliant birches was the river. The "chick-chee chick-chee" of snipe, the tinkle of willow warblers, and the loud rattle of a white-throat made the dawn chorus.

Unfortunately this brilliant spell was

short-lived. It soon turned to hail and rain showers as we made off up Glen Golly to walk its fascinating length. It is a lovely place of birches and mountain ash, and a river that runs through rocky walls. This spot is loved by pine martens, and although we did not see any, I am quite sure a few saw us. In a charmed corner of the glen we drummed up, with a fire of birch to boil our tea and eggs, before pushing on into the bare rocks of the hill pass to Dionard.

Rain met us on the pass, and in storms we climbed into this stony wilderness, to look down at last on Loch Dionard and its great crag. Up here we sat to watch the play of light on Meall Horn and Arkle, and speculate on possible routes up the massive face that lay before us, a thousand feet of it waiting to be explored.

This upper part of Strath Dionard is very heavy going for walkers, and we were glad after a mile or two to strike a track which led us to the promised hut whose location we had plotted on the map. Two camp beds, a little table, and a stove made up its furnishings, and the place was spotlessly clean. We lost no time in brewing up.

The stove must have been giving off paraffin fumes unfortunately, for I awoke next morning with a headache and a feeling of listlessness. The others complained of a similar feeling, which was a pity, for it was a marvellous morning with the sun shining and the river reflecting the rolling clouds. All the tops were showing off their fancy colours to great effect, but it was a crag marked A' Cheir Ghorm on the map which held our interest, a pyramid of grey rock offering a climb from the corrie floor to the crest of a narrow ridge.

Having breakfasted on trout, we made off to inspect that fine face at close quarters, but the rain beat us to it, and indeed snow was falling as we tied on the rope below the chosen start. It was bitter on the hands, and for the first hundred feet the going was very difficult indeed. It was too cold to continue on rock of this standard, so we traversed left to where the angle eased a bit, and reached the top by an interesting route.

Now that the climb was over, the weather began to improve. Below us Coire Duail with its ice-worn slabs was like a Cuillin corrie, while Loch Eriboll was blue as the glimpses of sky between drifting clouds. Shadows floated over the green patches by its shores, a contrast to the velvet grey of Conamheall and the wild rocks stretching to the face of Ben Hope and its snows. Away to the north the little gannet isle of Sule Stack was a shadow on the sea.

We made our way over the narrow ridge, rejoicing in the fine conditions. Lord Reay's Seat was a tooth of rock we had to visit, and from it we watched snow showers expend themselves to reveal the triple heads of Suilven, Quinag, Canisp, and in the far distance, An Teallach. West the high hills of Harris, and even the Cuillin, were visible on the vivid sea. Against this wonderful horizon, miles of silvery clouds floated. From Rudha Stoer to Eddrachillis Bay and Handa, the coast was just a mass of sparkling lochans and silhouettes of headlands and islands. Descending, we had a surprise encounter with an eagle, and had a view of the great bird from a distance of about 40 feet.

It was grand out of the wind that colourful evening. On the corrie floor, amongst the piled boulders, cushion pink and roseroot were blooming, particularly welcome for their delicate beauty in this otherwise sterile landscape.

I know of no other area in Scotland so barren of life—even the hoodie crow is absent from this glen. During a walk the following morning, I heard only a ring ouzel

Ben Hope and Loch Hope seen from the north. The 3040-feet mountain was one of the landmarks observed by Tom Weir on his spring expedition to Sutherland in the late 1940s.

PHOTO: TOM WEIR

calling from where a couple of rowan trees grew from some rocks. I saw three green-shank in courtship pursuit, two or three pairs of sandpipers, and a wheatear, meadow pipit and cuckoo. That was all. The only signs of spring in this place are the return of a few birds to the glen and the appearance of the little flowers of the bog—buck bean, lousewort, milkwort, tormentil, roseroot, and a few Alpines.

We packed, cleaned the bothy and cross-ed to Gualin House, where our depot of stores awaited our collection. We had never met the people, but they lost no time in providing us with tea, and all too soon we had to cut our ceilidh as the mail car drove up to take us to Keoldale, from where we were to ferry over the Kyle of Durness.

"Just wave a hankie," the car driver told us, "and the ferryman will be over for you." Standing waving a hankie across half a mile of water seemed a rather hopeless sort of business, but we did not grudge the wait, for after the rocky wilderness we had left, the green turf, fields and stone walls seemed delightfully inviting. Even the few houses put a different face on the land-scape.

As he was taking us across, the ferryman invited us to camp near his house, at a fine clearing on the edge of a birch gully above the sea. The trees and the chorus of bird-song made this spot very attractive, and soon we had the tents down, a floor of bracken laid, and a meal on the go.

Rain woke me during the night, but it dawned fine, so we were up and away early to go at last to Clo Mor. Our luck was in, for we got a lift by tractor to within a couple of miles of our cliffs. Beyond that, the road was impassable for wheeled vehicles and we said good-bye to our road repair party. The country around was unexciting, its gentle contours more like the Border hills.

Turning north, we followed the stream, knowing that a mile farther on we would come to the sea. Kearvaig Bay was as dramatic as the Clo Mor; a little curve of silver sand, a cottage, and beyond it rollers crashing in mushrooms of spray against rock skerries and cliffs. Kittiwake gulls were a fringe of white on a square-topped skerry, ring plovers ran about our feet, and on the sea were hundreds of swimming birds—eiders, razorbills, guille-mots, shags. The whole impression was of colour and movement, excitement and noise; blue sea and sky, silver spray, great cliffs of wine-red stone, and the beat of waves and the crying of birds.

At once we were among nesting birds. Puffins dodged out of burrows, scurrying away, black wings flickering, red legs hung out behind, and in front that remarkable ornament which can only be called a "beak," and not a very teetotal one, either! On the skerries and cliffs the ledges were crammed; razorbills on the lower tiers, fulmars on the upper, and everywhere, going in and out of burrows, puffins.

How can I convey the thrill of a coastline so full of movement that you can't take in any single portion at a glance? Standing on the edge of these cliffs, close on 1000 feet high, you are hypnotised by the very act of looking down. Birds criss-cross at so many different heights that you are almost com-pelled to join the rhythmic pattern. Look at them long enough and there is no knowing what might happen. Far below is the sea, churned to milk and showering columns of spray as the waves strike a half-submerged skerry. Nothing we meet on mountains is so frightening as the sheer plunge of those walls of Torridonian red sandstone.

This remarkable climate of ours! We spent a warm evening in the tent with a pleasant sunny morning following. Yet before breakfast was over, the temper-ature had dropped ten degrees or more, and hail was falling followed by heavy rain. We went exploring for birds, beginning with the hill Beinn an Amair and crossing the bog to Loch Airidh na Beinne, then down the Dall river. We saw no geese. A pair of greenshank, a few mallard, and an odd snipe rewarded our journey. To our disappointment we saw no snow bunting, geese, or pine marten.

We were looking forward to a closer acquaintance with Balnakeil Bay and the sands we had admired at a distance—as fine a sweep of white sand as there is in the whole of Scotland. A dozen whimbrel feed-ing there was something we did not expect to find. Later we were to see a small party of sanderlings almost on the same patch of sand, wanderers like the whimbrel, halting a little while before flying north to nest over the sea towards the midnight sun.

Then we came to the cliffs of this narrow headland, a miniature Clo Mor. Fulmars were everywhere and eggs or birds packed the ledges. It was good to see puffin burrows again, and a cliff full of kittiwakes. Under an overhang we could see a buz-zard's nest in a fearfully exposed place, a wonderful eyrie set dizzily above the crashing surf and half-submerged skerries.

On a little lochan was a gullery, a place of clustering marsh marigolds and buck bean. We took 19 eggs of the nesting black-headed gulls, feeling rather guilty about it, although we needed the food. Every burrow of this sandy soil seemed to contain a nesting wheatear.

By a spring of clear water we pitched our tents—too lovely a spot for our last night under canvas. In the dusk the rasping of corncrakes and the whirr of drumming snipe were comforting sounds, but carrying a portent of rain this cloudy night.

We packed up in a downpour to catch the mail-car south. On such a morning the run to Lairg was a desolation of boulders and tumbled rocks without grandeur. For more miles than you care to count, the country is bare of vegetation, peat banks laid out with newly-cut turfs being the only signs of human occupation. Little tracks and stony roads leading westwards to the fringe where the last lonely crofters live by the seashore indicated their destination.

The rich farms of Evanton and the green fields, Speyside and its wealth of trees, struck us as strange after the winter of Cape Wrath and the wild hills of Sutherland. ▮

WHAT THEY READ THEN

Edinburgh, Jan, 1770.
On Thursday, about seven o'clock at night, Newbattle-abbey, the seat of the Marquis of Lothian, about six miles south of Edinburgh, was discovered to be on fire. It made its first appearance in the north-east wing, towards the parks, but had got to such a height before it was discovered, that though every thing was done that could be done, there was no possibility of saving that part of the house. The fire burnt with prodigious violence till about two in the morning, when its fury was stopt by a strong party-wall, which gave an opportunity of saving part of the house.

The family were in the house at the time; they staid till about two, when my Lord and Lady came to town. The loss on this occasion must be very great. The fine pictures in the great gallery were all pulled down, and tossed over the windows, and suffered great damage; the library, the rich furniture of the principal apartments, and indeed almost every thing else, either suffered the same fate, or were consumed by the fire. In short, though it cannot yet be known, the loss to the family must be very great. A party of dragoons were sent for from Dalkeith, who were of great use in the occasion. No lives were lost.

During the fire, the following melancholy accident happened. One of the millers of Newbattle mills, on hearing the bell, ran to give his assistance. His wife, who was valetudinary, having gone to bed, he locked the door of his house after him. On his return, he found her dead, lying in the chimney. It would appear she had got up; that her fright had thrown her into a fit, to which she was often subject; and that unfortunately she had fallen into fire, where she was burnt to death.

From *The Scots Magazine*, February 1770.

WHAT THEY READ THEN

REMARKABLE ACCOUNT OF HIGHLAND ROBBERS

There is scarcely an instance of any country having made so sudden a chance in its moral as the Hebrides. Security and civility possess every part; yet sixty years have not elapsed since the whole was a den of thieves, of the most extraordinary kind. They conducted their plundering excursions with the utmost policy, and reduced the whole art of theft into a regular system. From habit it lost all the appearance of criminality: they considered it as labouring in their vocation; and when a party was formed for any expedition against their neighbour's property, they and their friends prayed as earnestly to heaven for success, as if they were engaged in the most laudible design.

The greatest crime was that of infidelity among themselves; the criminal underwent a summary trial, and, if convicted, never missed of a capital punishment. The chieftain had his officers, and different departments of government; he had his judge, to whom he instructed the decision of all civil disputes; but in criminal causes, the chief, assisted perhaps by some favourites, always undertook the process.

The principal men of his family, or his officers, formed his council, where everything was debated respecting their expeditions. Eloquence was held in great esteem among them; for by that they could sometimes work on their chieftain to change his opinion; for, notwithstanding he kept the form of a council, he always referred the decisive vote to himself.

When one man had a claim on another, but wanted power to make it good, it was held lawful for him to steal from his debtor as many cattle as would satisfy his demand, provided he sent notice, as soon as he got out of reach of pursuit, that he had them, and would return them, providing satisfaction was made on a certain day agreed on.

When a creach, or great expedition, had been made against distant herds, the owners, as soon as the discovery was made, rose in arms and, with all their friends, made instant pursuit, chasing the cattle by their track, for perhaps scores of miles. Their nicety in distinguishing that of their cattle from those that were only casually wandering or driven, was amazingly sagacious. As soon as they were arrived on an estate where the track was lost, they immediately attracted the proprietor, and would oblige him to discover the track from his land forwards, or to make good the loss they had sustained. This custom had the force of law, which gave to the Highlanders this surprising skill in the art of tracking.

It has been observed before, that to steal, rob, and plunder with dexterity, was esteemed as the highest act of heroism. The feuds between the great families was one great cause. There was not a chieftain but kept, in some remote valley, in the depths of woods and rocks, whole tribes of thieves in readiness to let loose against his neighbours, when, from some public or private reason, he did not judge it expedient to resent openly any real or imaginary affront. From this motive the greater chieftain-robbers always supported the lesser, and encouraged no sort of improvement on their estates but what promoted rapine.

From *The Scots Magazine*, April 1797.

HISTORY

THE FORGOTTEN WRECK

After she struck a reef off Foula in September 1914, the great liner Oceanic *lay on the sea-bed almost undisturbed until 1973.* **Simon Martin**, *who, along with his partner, rediscovered the vessel and carried out a salvage operation on her, tells here of how the wreck, for the second time, benefited the resourceful islanders.*

As the liner came into view, conversation died. The old men, who had been sitting hunched on the green headland outside the island's only shop, rose to their feet, took the pipes from their mouths, and stared in amazement. Not two miles off, the biggest ship they had ever seen loomed out of the mist, heading—as the island men knew only too well—straight for a reef of submerged rocks, half a mile of jagged black teeth.

They didn't have time to wonder why such a mighty vessel was here, so far from the shipping lanes, and so close to the shores of one of Britain's loneliest islands, the windswept emptiness of Foula, west of the Shetland mainland. For as the old men watched, a juddering roar sounded across the water—the steel plates of the liner being driven remorselessly on to the reef by the fast-flooding tide.

Mercifully she stayed upright, and soon scurrying figures could be seen swarming along the rail to lower lifeboats down the ship's tall sides. The Foula men ran for their own boats in nearby Ham Voe.

The ship was the 17,274-ton liner *Oceanic*, at her launch at Harland and Wolff, Belfast, in 1899, the world's biggest ship.

Now, in 1914, with the outbreak of the First World War, the *Oceanic* was temporarily on loan to the Royal Navy, and had been sent into northern waters to stop and search suspect shipping.

How she came to be stranded on Foula's notorious Hoevdi Reef—known locally as the Shaalds—was for a long time a source of embarrassment to the Royal Navy. Despite the fact that the sea was mirror-calm and the early morning Shetland mist had lifted, a series of navigational errors led the officers of the *Oceanic* to imagine they were somewhere completely different. By the time they realised their error, the sumptuous ship, with all her magnificent stained glass, gilt light fittings and painted panels, was hard aground.

In the days that followed, repeated Naval attempts to drag her clear of the reef came to nothing, and eventually the Foula men were pressed into service as emergency salvors of the ship's contents. To a community as isolated as Foula—with no other employment apart from the meagre livings from their crofts—this was an opportunity not to be missed. While they cheerfully helped the Navy to remove ammunition and guns from the stricken ship, they marvelled

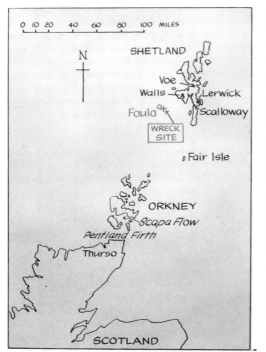

women were delighted with this bonanza, but not so pleased with the performance of their menfolk on the wreck on its final day on the reef. At the very last minute someone stumbled across the tobacco bond. Here were riches indeed! Pocketfuls of silverware and cutlery were instantly emptied and left to the sea—to the Foula men there was no contest—and they came ashore with as much tobacco as they could carry.

That night a heavy north-westerly gale blew up, and as darkness fell mighty seas crashed over the great ship. The following day there was nothing to be seen. The tobacco was soon smoked and the silverware was lost for ever—a point the Foula women were to put forcibly and frequently to their menfolk. Since the wind came from the north-west, treeless Foula could not even benefit much from deckwood washed up on the shore—most of it was driven across to the south-west corner of Shetland, where to this day crofters can point to furniture made by their grandfathers from high-quality *Oceanic* timber.

Soon the *Oceanic* faded from the headlines. Because of the remoteness of the site, the strength of the tide that sweeps the reef, and the unbroken ferocity of the seas—Foula is on the same latitude as Greenland and Leningrad and seas can build up from thousands of miles away before crashing and breaking on the Shaalds—the Admiralty decided it would be out of the question to try to recover the hundreds of tons of valuable non-ferrous metals from portholes to propellers which were fittings on the fine ship.

There was, however, a salvage attempt in the 1920s. The Scapa Flow Salvage and Shipbreaking Company was one of the first to work on the scuttled German First World War fleet in Orkney's sheltered anchorage where some truly amazing feats

at the floating palace soon to disappear under the sea. Think of it—first class cabins with marble lavatories, electric light, carved mahogany, and every conceivable luxury! On Foula, where no crofthouse had running water or sanitation— much less gas or electric light—these things were unheard of. The comparison with their own very simple crofthouses must have made the splendour of the former White Star Liner even more spectacular to the Foula men. As they moved about the ship the men picked up small items to "save from the sea". After all, what use was a good plate teapot or a brass doorknob at the bottom of the reef?

When they came ashore for the last time each day, every man's pockets bulged and clanked suspiciously as he climbed aboard the flit-boat—but the Naval officers turned a blind eye. In their crofthouses the Foula

The *Oceanic* in her heyday was the world's largest ship and one of the most luxurious.

PHOTO: HARLAND & WOLFF

took place. They bought the remains of the *Oceanic* from the Admiralty and sent their top diver, Robbie Robertson, out to the Shaalds.

His efforts only added weight to the story of the "undiveable" wreck. Kitted up in his traditional "hard hat" gear he was carefully lowered over the side of the island sixern. The fast-flowing tide caught both him and his air-line, and he streamed out to the stern of the boat. Within moments he was hauled aboard, exhausted and considerably distressed. His second diver refused even to go into the water. The project was abandoned almost before it had got under way.

The *Oceanic* was similar in many ways to that most famous of White Star liners, the ill-fated *Titanic*. Both in their heyday were the biggest ships in the world, their engine-room fittings (the real value in a wrecked steamship) were very similar, and many of the sailors wrecked with the *Oceanic* had suffered the same fate on the *Titanic* two years earlier. Yet amazingly while many dreamed of raising the *Titanic* from a totally impractical depth, her older sister lay completely forgotten in shallow water off a Scottish island for half a century.

Forgotten, that is, until two divers— Alec Crawford and myself—went to Foula in 1973 to visit the wreck site. With modern equipment it was just possible to dive during slack tide times, but we had to be patient, and over the next seven years we were able to dive on a total of only 200 days. As a result we had plenty of time to experience one of Scotland's most remote, least visited and beautiful islands.

Foula has no hotel, pub, or bed-and-breakfast croft, so visitors have to make plans in advance. Even the shop closed down during our years on the island. The laird's house, the Haa, which was usually unoccupied except for rare family visits, was made available to us. No major work had been done on the building since the film-makers of *The Edge of the World* (the story based on the evacuation of St Kilda, but filmed on Foula in 1936) had based themselves in the Haa.

As with the film people it was agreed that we should carry out repairs and maintenance work in lieu of rent. There was much to be done. There were perpetual puddles of water in the kitchen and living room, caused by water lying under the house in long-blocked drains. These had to be dug clear with pick and shovel. Smoke from the living-room fire poured, not up the chimney, but through the side of the wall and back into the room itself.

Once we began diving operations, the famous White Star liner again provided many valuable fittings for the island, as in the days of more than 60 years before when the *Oceanic* wallowed hopelessly on the reef. Not every piece of scrap hard-won from the Shaalds by us ended up in the metal merchant's yard. A visitor to the house today would notice a thick copper pipe serving as a lum for the stove in the kitchen—on the former Queen of the Seas it was a heavy steam pipe.

The smaller chintz stateroom on the *Oceanic*.

PHOTO: HARLAND & WOLFF

The Haa's new brass curtain rails—green with age and the chemical reaction from years under the sea—were segments cut from just two of thousands of tubes carefully loaded into the four massive 17-ton steam condensers in a Liverpool engineering yard at the end of the last century. They were held against the wall by brackets constructed from copper drawn from several tons extracted from the ship's generators.

When the smoke-belching fire was reconstructed, fire bricks from a ship's boiler were used. Our only hot water came from a heavy cast-iron kettle placed on the peat-burning fire, and when this boiled it was placed for safety on a 32 lb. brass nut which had once helped to fasten one of the ship's towering 29-ton propellers. Incidentally, no coal was burned on Foula while we were on the island—the only exceptions being when, for fun, a diver would bring up a couple of lumps from the wreck of a ship which at peak speed burned an incredible 700 tons each day!

Outside the house, too, many *Oceanic* materials were used. The roof had been slated 100 years previously and not surprisingly—in view of the ferocious gales that frequently hit the island—the slates often came loose. They were carefully wired back into position using copper which had once been generator windings.

The house's water was collected in a tank via gutters on the edge of the roof. We soon put up a second tank, and connected it to the system with a gunmetal valve which had been one of hundreds on the two triple-expansion, four-cylinder steam engines—a valve in such fine condition that even after 60 years of battering under the sea it still carried the grease applied by an engineer in 1914.

Outside the Haa, *Oceanic* fittings began to find a use in everyday life on Foula once

more. When valves and pumps salvaged from the wreck were stripped down to their basic metals—essential if top prices are to be commanded—we used to put the small brass nuts, bolts, washers and other small fittings into a bin and encouraged anyone on the island to make use of them when the need arose. As scrap they would be of negligible value, but in a community far from the ironmonger's store or the spare parts centre, they were often vital to get a piece of machinery working again. Our own van ran complete with an *Oceanic* spare—a Heath Robinson type adaptation to the handbrake—and to my knowledge a tractor and generator still run with parts first put into the White Star liner in Belfast last century.

The list goes on. A Shetland craftsman who specialised in making scripted name-plates from copper strips found the *Oceanic's* generator strapping much purer and easier to work with than his normal present-day supplies. The Foula fishermen would often lose their weighted hand-lines along the undulating rock reef, and new weights, or doros as they are called in Shetland, were constantly needed. They would soon fashion them from pieces of our lead bilge piping and get back to "drawing the piltocks." *Oceanic* lead was also manufactured on the island into pellets for shotgun cartridges.

Steel piston heads, uneconomic to ship south, but which nonetheless had to be lifted to get at the brass liners, were not dumped at sea but eagerly accepted by crofters to hold down the nets on their coles of hay. Our own salvage boats used several *Oceanic* pieces of metal once more—a compass-light holder for example—and copper ornamentation found its way on to several of the small island boats.

Some of the *Oceanic* brass became ornaments and souvenirs. When my partner Alec and his wife Moya were married on the isle in 1976—the first island wedding since the 1940s—among the many fine presents they received was a tray made out of one of the few bits of *Oceanic* timber washed ashore in 1914. The tray was even decorated with highly polished and engraved *Oceanic* copper.

We recovered two heavy gunmetal bowls with the White Star flag embossed on them. We never really worked out what they were—perhaps they were ashtrays. That's certainly what they are now! In addition to propellers, condensers and pumps—we recovered a record-breaking near-250 tons of non-ferrous metals from the one-time "undiveable ship"—we also recovered the chef's kettle, his tea-urn, a bowl and a much-crumpled patty tin. They were all copper—what a sight his galley must have been—but sadly were damaged almost beyond recognition.

To the people of Foula the wrecking of the *Oceanic* was more than just the loss of a magnificent ship. On two occasions—with more than half a century separating them—the wreck has been the source of very welcome materials to make life on the island a little bit easier. Even today the islanders face a period of several weeks completely cut off from the outside world each winter, when neither plane nor boat can reach them easily. In these circumstances many generations of Foula people have become accustomed to making the most of every tiny opportunity—a fish-box washed up in a small geo, metal from a crashed aeroplane or a piece of floating netting for their creels. The *Oceanic* was merely the jackpot.

Over the peat stove many households still hang racks of dried fish and "risted" mutton—the fish probably caught by the young fishermen on the Shaalds during the summer. Although Foula does not have much snow, the island frequently experiences winds of quite unbelievable ferocity. Our first salvage boat was smashed to matchwood in a few minutes at Ham Voe as a result of mountainous seas whipped up by a Shetland gale. The wind was so fierce we could barely stand up in it, but even that was nothing to one 150-knot blow which flattened a stone building, turned a tractor completely upside-down, and whisked away almost every haystack on the island; one turned up, still intact, more than 20 miles away on the Shetland mainland!

Over the years our work has taken us round many of the Scottish islands, but Foula is unique. Towering out of the sea, the west side boasts some of the most spectacular high cliffs in Britain. As the seaborne visitor approaches from the east, the five main peaks of The Noup, Hamnafjeld, The Sneug, The Kame and Soberlie Hill rise up stark and sheer—the size of the island accentuated by its very isolation.

The 40 or so inhabitants live a hard, lonely and often bleak life. A considerable portion of their income is derived from the huge numbers of wiry and almost completely wild brown and black Shetland sheep which roam the unfenced hillside, often eluding all attempts at capture for several years at a time. Another source of income is knitting, an ideal money-making pastime for a wife at home with young children. Many standard views of economics are overturned by the Foula way of life, where an old-age pensioner can be quite well-off bearing in mind that the rent will be only a few pounds a year, electricity, coal, gas and transport bills are non-existent, and there is no shop or hotel in which to spend money.

Visitors often make the mistake of equating this simple way of life with a simple people. The cleric from a passing

Alec Crawford *(left)* and Simon Martin with one of the *Oceanic's* propeller blades which they salvaged from the wrecked liner.

A dangerous task during the salvage operation. A diver lays an explosive charge inside the casing of one of the four 17-ton brass condensers. The charge will open the casing, freeing the 3,000-or-so brass tubes inside.   PHOTO: SIMON MARTIN

cruise ship who condescendingly pressed 5p into the hand of a young barefoot island woman tending her sheep would have been astounded to learn that she possessed a university degree probably better than his own. Young islanders leave Foula for their last years at school, often travelling south to university before making the positive decision to come back home.

Because of the remoteness of the island, local traditions on Foula are still much to the fore. Many of the remoter places in

Scotland still pay lip service to the old Julian Calendar, but Foula genuinely celebrates Old Yule on January 6 and New Year on the 13th. As a result it's not unheard of for children to be at their school desks on December 25, though, as one island woman put it: "We sometimes just have two Christmases and two New Years!"

Initially we were often confused when the old men told us that we could expect good diving weather at the beginning of May—they were in fact meaning mid-May to our way of thinking. The calendar has been changed for centuries now, but Foula has a strong sense of tradition.

The island was also the last place in Britain to speak Old Norse—at the beginning of last century—and one thing we had to get used to was the Shetland names for the hundreds of thousands of birds that visit each year. The island is the biggest breeding ground in the world for the bonxies (great skuas), while nories (puffins), terricks (terns), maalies (fulmars), peerie mooties (storm petrels), lung-wees (razorbills), scarfs (shags), dunters (eiders), swaabies (black-backed gulls) and a host of other birds make Foula an ornithologist's dream.

In days goneby, as on St Kilda, the seabirds' eggs and often the birds themselves formed an important part of the island diet. The young men were lowered over the sheer cliffs on ropes, carrying a basket and a scoop on the end of a pole, and in this way they plundered the nests. Many of the islanders are still incredibly agile on the cliffs. One day I happened to mention to John Andrew Ratter, a Foula man who worked with us on the Shaalds, that I would

like a close-up photograph of some of the birds. Without a word he leapt over the edge of the cliffs, landed on a tiny ledge some 15 feet below, stuffed an astonished bird under each arm, and climbed swiftly back to the top using his elbows for leverage! One false step and he would have fallen hundreds of feet to the rocks and sea below.

Everyone in Shetland is rightly concerned about the consequences to this unique wealth of wildlife, should one of the giant tankers plying to and from Sullom Voe be wrecked. Reputedly, one narrowly missed the Shaalds more by luck than judgement, and a few small spills have already taken a dreadful toll of birds, seals, otters and even sheep. The *Oceanic*—still Shetland's biggest wreck by a long way— was undoubtedly a catastrophe to the Royal Navy so soon after the start of the war, but at least she caused no problems when she broke up and brought a small bonus to a very poor community. The next great ship to run on to the rocks in Shetland—and judging by the near misses it will be "when" rather than "if"—will be a disaster for everyone without exception. ◼

DISASTER AT QUINTINSHILL

Hugh Dougherty recalls the circumstances of the United Kingdom's worst railway accident.

The papers were full of war news in May 1915. The Dardanelles Campaign was getting well under way. In April, Sir Ian Hamilton had made an attack, while plans were in full swing to bring about the landing at Sulva Bay, timed for August. All over Scotland, men were volunteering to enlist, for it was still a volunteer war in May 1915, and half a battalion of the 7th Royal Scots were looking forward to finishing their training, and making the journey to exotic Turkey.

All from around Leith, the men and officers had worked hard for the day when they could serve their country, for such was the depth of pro-war feeling in early summer that year. There was jubilation when news reached their training ground at Stenhousemuir that they were to leave on 19th May, by troop train from Larbert, for Liverpool, where a ship was waiting to take them on the most exciting journey of their lives.

Had the 15 officers and 470 men made that journey on the date planned, they would probably have left very little mark on history, but, because of a rolling stock shortage, the Caledonian Railway had to postpone their journey until 22nd May—a date now remembered as the most tragic in the history of Scottish railways. Quintinshill, just outside Gretna, was as far as the proud Royal Scots got on that fateful troop train, thanks to the laxity of a signalman, James Tinsley, who put the name of his signalbox on the map of history for ever. His series of errors accounted for the staggering total of 227 killed, and 246 injured.

It was a tragic combination of circumstances which led to the Gretna disaster. When, at 6.24 a.m., Tinsley reported for duty at his box at Quintinshill on that sunny May morning 74 years ago, everything seemed in order, and it looked like being a normal day shift. In fact, Tinsley was late. He ought to have started work at 6.00 a.m. For some time, however, he'd been in the habit of getting a highly unofficial lift on the engine of the 6.10 local from Carlisle to Beattock, which picked him up at Gretna station, where he lived in a railway cottage.

Tinsley's partner in crime was night shift man George Meakin, who agreed to his colleague arriving half an hour late on the local, thus letting him get a ride up the line. They had an arrangement, possibly known to local officials, that allowed Tinsley to fill up, in his own hand, the train register—the official record of all activity in the signalbox—from 6.00 a.m., by copying entries from notes made by Meakin on a piece of paper.

They had probably been doing this quite successfully for years, and, with Tinsley's newspaper arriving with him, there was time for a quick flick through it and a chat on the progress of the war and other matters. Such brief social exchanges were by no means uncommon in the isolated signalboxes regulating the traffic up and down the important railway between Glasgow and Carlisle, for there was little enough human contact during the long ten-hour shifts with only the signalling bells and telephone for company.

However, everything was to go horrifically wrong on 22nd May, for on that day Tinsley was being called on to handle five trains through his section, both north to Kirkpatrick, and south to Gretna. From the north, a train of empty coal wagons was making for Carlisle, having delivered its load to naval bases; also making its way south with great speed, and catching up on the coal train, was the troop train from Larbert, carrying the ill-fated Royal Scots.

Steaming northwards was the sleeper from London, with its portions for Glasgow and Edinburgh, while already in Tinsley's northbound loop line, was the 4.50 goods train from Carlisle. The local on which he had arrived stood outside the box on the northbound main line.

His task was clear. He had to allow the troop train and the sleeper to pass, and to do that, he would have to clear the main lines, both north and south, by using his loop sidings on both sides of the tracks. Tragically, he carried out the various

The aftermath of the catastrophic Quintinshill rail crash in May 1915. Following the collision fire destroyed much of what remained as shown by the charred skeleton of this once elegant 12-wheeled coach. PHOTO: BBC HULTON PICTURE LIBRARY

movements incorrectly, breaking several very important rules in the process, and creating a situation that sealed the fate of the local, the troop train and the sleeper.

The major blunder was reversing the local train on to the southbound main line to let the sleeper through and then, amazingly, forgetting about it. The coal train in the loop was out of the way of the troop train, but the local had taken its place. The rules were then disobeyed, for the signalman at Kirkpatrick was not informed that the southbound main line was occupied—a procedure known as "blocking back", which would have ensured that the troop train would have been held at the signals outside Quintinshill.

Tinsley was not entirely to blame, however, for it seems that it was Meakin who actually made these initial mistakes, and went on to compound them, and seal the fate of all concerned, by breaking a further rule through failing to put a "collar" on the levers of the signals protecting the local train. A collar is a small cast iron ring, which a signalman is required to slip over the release lever of signals set at danger to protect a train left standing on the main line. If he subsequently tries to release the signals, he is prevented from doing so, and an accident is avoided.

Meakin ignored that rule, probably as Tinsley got busy forging the entries in the train register, so that when Tinsley got word from Kirkpatrick that the troop train was coming into his section, he accepted it, and pulled off the very signals which would have prevented it coming any farther. One small cast iron ring would have saved the day.

So it was that, at 6.49, the troop train, dashing for the Border at around 60 m.p.h. packed with the Royal Scots anxious for their first glimpse of England, charged round the bend into Quintinshill and rammed the local with such force that both engines virtually disintegrated. The 15 coaches of the troop train all but collapsed, too, particularly the leading vehicles, for all were ancient wooden-bodied affairs, pressed into service because of the heavy wartime traffic.

Tinsley and Meakin looked out of their box in disbelief, but the worst was yet to come, for, at 6.50, just one minute later,

the sleeper, pounding north from Carlisle, crashed into the wreckage with a second mighty roar, adding to the carnage already evident. Nobody would forget what happened next, for hot coals from the engines set fire to the ruptured tanks which supplied oil-gas for carriage lighting, and the Gretna holocaust was alight.

The flames caught easily, for the wooden-bodied coaches had been reduced to firewood by the impact of the collisions. Railmen still able to help were beaten back by the flames. It was a horrible business, for they could hear trapped soldiers crying for help as the flames roared towards them. Attempts were made to use water left in the engines' tenders, but that was in vain, and the fire sent a huge pall of funereal smoke high above Quintinshill on that still summer morning.

Word was sent to Carlisle at 7.14, where

Hundreds of dying and injured soldiers were treated in the lineside fields.

District Traffic Superintendent Blackstock organised a special rescue train, with doctors and railwaymen. Because of an incredible oversight, the Carlisle fire brigade received word of the disaster far too late, and it was well after nine o'clock before any effective fire fighting took place, by which time the blaze was well beyond control. It burned for almost 24 hours.

Local people and railwaymen, assisted by passengers from the sleeper, and those soldiers fit enough, worked long and hard together to pull the injured from the wreckage. Doctors performed on-the-spot amputations to get men out before the flames reached them, and the resulting streams of injured and burned arriving in Carlisle all day after the accident, stretched the medical services to the limit. There had simply never been a disaster on this scale.

Naturally, the Press descended on the scene, for here was sensation in plenty. There was the tragedy of the human loss to report, and there was the added dimension of the deaths of brave men on their way to war. There was public shock that something as permanent and safe as the mighty Caledonian Railway could actually kill so many people, and there was the Press campaign against poor Tinsley, whose moments of forgetfulness had turned both himself and Meakin into criminals.

When the totals were finally drawn up, the papers stunned the whole nation by stating the awful facts: 227 people were dead. Of the soldiers killed, 83 were recognisable, and 82 were so badly burned that they could not be identified, while a further 50 were never traced. They had been totally consumed by the flames, and, here and there in the grim wreckage, reporters recalled seeing small pieces of melted metal which had once been uniform buckles or buttons. It seemed inconceivable that the military pride of Scotland could be killed during something so mundane as a railway journey on Scottish soil, but there was no escaping the terrible facts.

Those facts were brought to the very doorstep of the people of Leith on 24th May, when the Royal Scots were buried in Rosebank Cemetery. The funeral procession took over three hours to pass on its way to the final resting place of the men who came home so unexpectedly soon. There were other funerals, of railwaymen killed in the crash, and of sleeping car passengers. Sorrow turned to public anger when official enquiries went ahead into the tragedy. Tinsley and Meakin were arrested, to suffer the ordeal of a Coroner's Inquest at Carlisle, although the accident had taken place on the other side of the Border. They finally stood trial on 24th September 1915 in the Edinburgh High Court.

Also standing trial was George Hutchinson, fireman of the fateful local, who should have insisted that the vital lever collar was put in place to ensure his train's protection. All three were charged with killing those who perished.

It was over quickly, and the jury retired at 12.40, returning at 12.48 to give their findings to Lord Strathclyde. Hutchinson was not guilty, but Meakin and Tinsley were. The verdict was unanimous, and Tinsley was sentenced to three years in prison, with Meakin getting half that figure. Public justice was done, though there were those in railway service who felt the sentences were harsh, as both men had otherwise perfect records of faithful service to their highly-respected employers.

After they had served their sentences, Tinsley later rejoined the railway as a lampman at Carlisle, a job which must have acted as a constant reminder of that awful morning in 1915. He died in 1967, occasionally hounded by some reporter anxious to interview the man who caused Scotland's greatest railway disaster. Meakin did not rejoin the railway. He died in obscurity in the mid-Fifties.

Today, there are few visible signs of the events that terrible morning at Quintinshill except the poignant memorial to the men of the Royal Scots in Leith's Rosebank Cemetery, and a bulging file in West Register House. The headlines of papers on microfilm in Glasgow's Mitchell Library still scream their story in bold type, so that something of the numb shock that gripped the reader of 1915 can still be felt today.

Quintinshill box was demolished in the early Seventies when new colour light signals were introduced. They are control-led from Motherwell and Carlisle. The passenger of today would be hard put to catch a glimpse of Quintinshill, although there are still loop sidings, and the men who run the line are all very much aware of what happened there in the days of their grandfathers.

The appalling story has been passed down through generations of railwaymen, and they are unlikely to forget, like poor Tinsley, who, for one moment on 22nd May 1915, ignored the cardinal rule of all railway operating—constant vigilance is the price of safety—and thus was responsible for the most terrible railway disaster that Britain has ever seen. ▣

THE FIRST MacDONALD MASSACRE

Euan McIlwraith recalls a grim chapter in clan history.

The Massacre of Glencoe has established itself firmly in our folklore. It is also, probably, the best-known slaughter in the world.

On that occasion, men, women and children of the Clan Donald lost their lives at the hands of the Campbells. This cruel act has become important in the history of the MacDonalds, but in terms of numbers, it is dwarfed by an earlier event. In 1577 the entire community of Eigg was wiped out in one horrific act of barbarism.

The island lies to the south of Skye, and forms part of the chain of Canna, Rum, Eigg and Muck. The MacDonalds of Clanranald populated Eigg at that time, a branch of the all-powerful MacDonalds, Lords of the Isles.

There existed, then, a feud between the McLeods of Skye and the MacDonalds, over disputed lands in Skye, so it was with no great feelings of brotherhood that a party of McLeods in the early spring of 1577, landed on Eilean Chathastial, an islet just off the southern corner of Eigg.

A small number of women were tending cattle there and the story goes that one of the women was assaulted by a McLeod. Her companions' cries were heard on Eigg, and their own menfolk arrived just as the Skye men were preparing to leave. A short skirmish took place which resulted in the McLeods being bound hand and foot and set adrift in their boat. It was a callous act considering the wild seas at that time of year.

Legend also has it that the hands were cut off the McLeod who had attacked the woman.

The McLeods drifted until they managed to free themselves, then sped home with stories of unprovoked assault and exaggeration of the numbers of MacDonalds involved.

This is where the accounts differ, depending on which family history you follow, for both sides claim to be innocent.

Incensed by the tale brought back, the McLeods mustered a war party and set sail for Eigg.

The MacDonalds, expecting retaliation, had posted a lookout, and the McLeod galleys were spotted as they approached the northern shore. A hasty conference took place. It was decided that it would be safer to hide, rather than risk defeat by the superior McLeod forces.

All members of the clan were called and they made for the south of the island where they sought the safety of Uamh Fhraing: the Cave of St Francis. This is a long narrow cavern, with a slit entrance which widens to form a chamber 70 yards long by six wide. Into this long dark hole, just under 400 men, women and children, crept and sat huddled together to protect themselves against the cold. The men stayed at the mouth with the intention of preventing entry, if the hiding place was discovered.

The McLeods landed and searched the island, but to no avail. In their frustration they looted the homes of the islanders and put the buildings to the torch.

The terrified MacDonalds crouched in the dampness of the cave for many hours, and eventually, not having been discovered, felt they were safe.

They decided to send someone to check, but the man selected was dismayed to find that snow had fallen during the day and that any footprints would lead to the hiding place. It's said that he walked backwards to hide the direction of the cave, but this has a false ring to it as any footprints would obviously have aroused suspicion amongst the invaders.

The Eigg man discovered that the McLeods were in the process of leaving and that the MacDonalds would very soon be safe. It was then the islander made the fatal mistake which was to cost not only his own life, but that of his friends and relations.

Instead of hiding where he was until all was safe, he retraced his steps to bring the joyful news to the others. He was spotted by a lookout on one of the departing galleys, and the boats turned and landed where the scout had last been seen.

They found his footprints, but the MacDonald had waded along the shore when he got close to the cave to avoid detection, and had followed a stream bed to the cave mouth. However, the McLeods searched every inch of the shoreline until a shout from one of the searchers told that the secret of the cave was out.

The problem of how to storm it had yet to be solved; as the mouth was so small, only one man could enter at a time. This gave a decided advantage to the defenders, who could slay each McLeod as he crawled in.

The MacDonalds waited nervously for the attack which never came. Just when they were beginning to believe that the McLeods had given up, they heard the crackling of a fire. Their earlier complacency turned to horror as billows of smoke began to fill the cave, and realisation dawned on them.

The screams of the MacDonalds must have been horrifying, but at last the rocky tomb fell silent. The McLeods returned to Skye where they were greeted as heroes.

The story of the Massacre of Eigg has

The narrow entrance to the cave in which the MacDonalds died.   PHOTO: TOM WEIR

been handed down to this generation, subject to exaggeration, alterations and embellishments depending on which family you believe.

The McLeods have two versions. In one they were the victims of an unprovoked attack and so were justified in their revenge, while in the other, they blame the MacLeans of Duart and the survivors of the Spanish ship sunk in Tobermory Bay in the 1580s. This force did indeed raid Muck, Rum, Eigg and Canna in 1588. The tales of cruelty and pillage on this expedition would fit in well with the legend.

As there were no survivors, it is quite possible that no one really knew the true perpetrators of the crime. It is highly likely that a blend of fact and the well-known existence of the McLeod feud, has led to the story as it is today.

It is said that the remains of the bodies were discovered last century and that the bones were removed and given a Christian burial.

The facts of the massacre are vague and the location of the mass grave unknown, but the persistence of the legend in Mac-Donald folklore suggests that some trag-

Billows of smoke began to fill the cave.

CHARLES BANNERMAN

edy did in fact take place in that lonely cave.

It is sad to think that the same clan was doomed to suffer again in Glencoe, just 115 years later.

WHAT THEY READ THEN

THE DEATH OF ROBERT BURNS

At Dumfries, after a lingering illness, the celebrated Robert Burns. His poetical compositions, distinguished equally by the force of native humour, by the warmth and the tenderness of passion, and by the glowing touches of a descriptive pencil, will remain a lasting monument of the vigour and the versatility of a mind guided only by the lights of nature and the inspirations of genius.

His ordinary endowments, however, were accompanied with frailties which rendered them useless to himself and his family. The last months of his short life were spent in sickness and indigence; and his widow, with five infant children, and in the hourly expectation of a sixth, is now left without any resource, but what she may hope from the regard due to the memory of her husband.

From *The Scots Magazine*, July 1796.

J

WHAT THEY READ THEN

TO THE EDITOR OF *THE SCOTS MAGAZINE*

Sir,

I beg leave to offer you a few hints which I think will greatly improve your publication; for which I am sure all your female readers will thank me, and several gentlemen, too, who like me, are obliged to become your readers. Pardon the expression, Sir, for I must own that the *Lady's Magazine* is much more to my liking; but my aunt, with whom I live, is like you, sometimes too wise to be agreeable, and she has lately taken it into her head, to give it up, and take to yours, thinking, as she says herself, that there ought to be no sex in books, but that they ought to be calculated for the species, rather than for particular parts of it.

I own I was much disappointed in the chance, for pardon me, Mr. Editor, I think you are too dry and too deep for female capacities; instead of giving us the newest fashions, or telling us what is going on in the gay world, you tell us only of a parcel of savages, their barbarous customs, and a country that nobody ever heard of before; of books which nobody can make anything of; of these vile French which one is weary hearing of, with a parcel of long debates, which no one cares about, or will be at the trouble to read.

It is true, you promised to enliven your work in future with engravings of eminent men; I hope you do not mean a parcel of old grey-beards, but that I shall be able to recognise some of my acquaintances among them, such as Sir Harry Hound, Tom Trip, Lord Stare etc etc. I shall only now offer you a few hints, which I hope you will profit by, and not make your book as tiresome as one of Tillotson's sermons, which is read as duly in our family every Sunday night, as your magazine is every month.

In the first place, I would have you begin with a particular description of the fashions, new trimmings, colours, etc. with what figure and complexion suits them best; then I would have a sweet story or two, I have seen the *Lady's Magazine* have three going on at the same time, besides episodes, and anecdotes; then two pages of divine poetry; an account of the new plays, operas, and dramatic pieces; if you could insert the music of the latter, it would be a great addition; and then finish with the deaths and marriages, which will much oblige all your female readers, and particularly

Lydia Lapwing

. . .

We are sorry our sprightly correspondent, Miss Lapwing, should find nothing to interest her in our miscellany; we have inserted her letter verbatim, and like many good hearers of advice, turn its application from ourselves to others, namely, to parents who have daughters to educate; why, we would ask, is their attention confined merely to the trifles of a day, dress and fashion, music and dancing, by which, the mind, instead of being improved, is narrowed and degraded, or left a blank without one rational, or general idea?

Surely nothing that is pleasing in education, no polite accomplishment, should be deemed trifling, or below a woman's attention; but may not these be combined with what is more solid and permanent, with instructive and general reading? It is the accomplished mind, which constitutes the lasting charms of a woman, and fits her to be the companion of man's happiest hours.

After all, notwithstanding our gravity, we shall be glad of the future correspondence of this lively lady, and shall do our utmost to gratify her taste, even in the exhibition of a pattern.

From *The Scots Magazine*, February, 1801.

I REMEMBER

WHEN I WAS IN PANTO

Florence Tudor

Though the old Princess Theatre may change its face,
Its heart aye remains in the very same place.

Over 40 years have passed, but I can still remember The Guv'nor standing stiff and straight, expression severe, yet counteracted by an almost unobserved twinkle in his eye, repeating that little rhyme to a trembling would-be Principal Girl. I was that girl, and Harry McKelvie, late owner of The Royal Princess's Theatre at Gorbals Cross in old Glasgow, The Guv'nor.

As I came to know Mr McKelvie better, I appreciated he was a strict disciplinarian who demanded, and got, the best from his cast, along with their respect and obedience. Hence his ever-successful pantomimes.

Variety was indeed the spice of life in those days of crowded theatres, appreciative audiences and happy-go-lucky artistes, to whom the feel of the boards and the smell of the greasepaint meant more than life itself.

I was one of that band of ever-hopeful artistes. I think at birth a Good Fairy must have waved her magic wand, thereby bestowing upon me an inordinate love of the footlights, for their attraction has been inescapable throughout my life.

Harry McKelvie was revered in theatreland. To be given a role in any of his pantomimes meant you had arrived, so, when I received a letter asking me to call and meet him in William Galt's Variety Agency in Sauchiehall Street, I complied with alacrity—and a trembling heart.

I was informed by Nellie Sutherland whose job it was to arrange the booking of artistes, that the Guv'nor in person was coming to the office that morning. Now, the Guv'nor, as he was invariably called, meant nothing to me at that time and I said so in a disappointed voice, for hadn't I been asked to report for a proposed role in the Princess's Pantomime?

"Florence," remarked a scathing Nellie, "don't you realise you are speaking about *the* Mr Harry McKelvie of the Princess's Theatre? *He* is the Guv'nor." I felt like a pricked balloon and only wished the ground would open up and swallow me. How could I have been so stupid?

Luckily for me, however, Mr McKelvie had not yet put in an appearance, and I was given a most important piece of advice to add to my worries.

"If he should consider you, do not, whatever you do, mention the word 'contract'."

It transpired that the Guv'nor's word was his bond, and anyone demanding the customary contract would find him or herself barred for life from his pantomimes. Thus, when the great man arrived, looked me over, then barked, "If I engaged you as Principal Girl, would you want a contract?" I smilingly returned his gaze saying, "Cer-

[131]

tainly not, sir. Should you decide I'm suitable for the part you have in mind, that is good enough for me."

His retort was to tell me I had got the role—and that I would be expected to provide my own costumes!

The Princess's Pantomime was an institution in Glasgow. Its shows were the longest-running in the country, lasting well after the first crocus had reared its head, and our audiences came from far and near prepared to make a meal of it—in more ways than one, for they would be armed with sandwiches, fruit, sweets and cold drinks. In fact anything for eating to sustain them through a show which could last for up to five hours.

The chief comic was George West, known and loved by thousands. A clean, wholesome comedian, George wouldn't have cracked a risqué gag to save his life, and his fund of humour more than satisfied the families for whom he could do no wrong. He was very intelligent and although essentially quiet and reserved had a droll sense of humour off stage. His spontaneous bursts of wit were thoroughly enjoyed, and I can still visualise him, tall and burly, striding around in the most outrageous costumes, with a comical red wig stuck on his head.

George West loved children, and they, sensing this, adored him for it.

His feeds were Jack E. Raymond, slender, dapper and sophisticated, the antithesis of George, and wee Nellie Forbes, a plump, earthy comedienne with an inexhaustible fund of witty stories, who used to keep her audiences in stitches with her many and humorous ditties.

Nellie was the perfect foil for George and was at all times "mother" to the entire cast. Everyone went to her with their troubles, and her advice was sound and always concluded with a sympathetic pat on the head. She was one of the old school, and would have carried on working until she dropped. I learned a great deal about life with its ups and downs from that lady.

My first solo spot in the pantomime was when I sang "My Heart Awakes When April Sings". A very appropriate ballad, for, when April did arrive, we were still playing to capacity audiences!

For the first time in my life I had my very own dressing room with a cosy little fire. The latter was definitely welcome after years of chilly theatre accommodation. What gave me a real sense of importance, however, was the fact that I had my own dresser, Patsy by name. Patsy was well versed in the peculiarities of stage folk, and a decided asset when it came to quick changes, for I had so many dainty costumes which had to be carefully taken off, washed and ironed ready for each performance.

We played a considerable number of matinée performances, and Patsy never failed to bring me something tasty for tea, as artistes were not permitted to go outside the theatre between shows. There was a small couch in the dressing room, and she always insisted I rest there until the evening performance. I wouldn't have changed places with the Queen when my small table was placed beside me, carefully set with an appetising meal, followed by a huge cream cake. Patsy knew my weakness!

There is something comforting about feeling just that little bit important, and my mother was so proud when she paid her respects to a daughter who could boast about her very own dressing room. Would that one could turn the clock back for just one day. These were such happy times.

Jeanette Adie was Principal Boy, and eminently suited to that role. In Variety, she did a male impersonator act, immaculately dressed in perfectly tailored suits,

Florence Tudor as she was at the time of her reminiscences.

and she made a captivating "Boy" in pantomime. Many were the times, on stage with her, when it took a supreme effort not to laugh outright at the outrageous jokes she would whisper in my ear during our passionate love duets.

My greatest worry was when I had to perform the few steps which constituted our dance routine, for never have I professed to be a dancer. Although Jeanette carefully guided me, I became more and more nervous at rehearsal, certain everyone present thought I had two left legs. It was then the Guv'nor barked, "I didn't engage this girl for her feet, it's her voice I'm interested in." His words were the boost I needed, and our dance went through without a hitch.

These were the moments which endeared one to Harry McKelvie. He had the gift of transforming his show into one for the entire family, was always concerned with the welfare of his cast, and was scrupulously fair in his dealings. A man who invited, and received, implicit trust.

One of his idiosyncracies was that the titles of his pantomimes all contained 13 letters. This one was "Tammy Twinkle". Evidently he was out to defy superstition.

Hope Jackman was our Dandini (although the pantomime bore no resemblance whatsoever to "Cinderella"). She was the only English artiste in the cast and it took her some time to adjust to the Scots, but everyone tried to make her feel at home, although I don't believe she ever understood George West's sense of humour. I never again heard of her playing in a Scottish pantomime, but, within recent years, have seen her on television. Obviously she is still keeping her hand in.

The Scottish brand of pawky humour is a style unto itself, but no-one can deny that our comedians possess the knack of making even the least appreciative audience not only smile, but roar with laughter—and a good laugh never hurt anyone.

Twice during the run of the pantomime, I saw the guardian of the theatre, the ghostly figure who regularly appeared—though only in successful seasons.

In the first instance, I was preparing to go on stage during our first Saturday matinée, when I observed, walking slowly in front of me, the tall figure of a man, dressed in a dark, flowing robe, with a kind of girdle round his waist. He was thin, stooped a little, kept his head down, and had long straight hair. Knowing Jack E. Raymond's weakness for playing tricks, I shouted, "Wait for me, Jack. What's the idea of dressing up for Hallowe'en?" There was no reply. The figure never turned its head, so I quickened my footsteps, but, before I reached the apparition, it vanished. As far as I could make out, allowing for my amazement, it appeared to walk through a door leading to the stage.

Racing back to Jack Raymond's dressing room, I blurted out the story to him. He said nothing, but took my arm and led me through the door and on to the stage. At the end of the performance he explained about the figure. Apparently it had first made its appearance as far back as 1878 when the theatre was opened as Her Majesty's.

The mystery figure was known as "Pepper's Ghost" after the title of a drama produced at the theatre after its opening. Jack also told me it appeared only if the run of a pantomime was to prove successful.

I was told that it must at all times be regarded as a friend, and that all it had been known to do was to walk slowly around the corridors.

Jack Raymond also quoted the following rhyme to me which was supposed in those days to refer to Pepper's Ghost, and its evident interest in the theatrical artistes:

*Come sit doon, auld cronies, an gie me
   your crack.
Let the win tak the cares o this life on its
   back,
Our herts tae despondency we ne'er will
   submit,
For we've aye been provided for, an
   saw will we yet.*

The second time I saw the figure was from my dressing room when it glided past the open door. I couldn't make out the face, for it appeared to be looking at the floor. Although I appreciated being told it never actually paid attention to anyone, I always had an uneasy feeling going on stage, but never again did I set eyes on our guardian. However, its appearance did indeed herald a record-breaking run. In this particular season we played for well over six months.

The production ran riot at all performances. We never knew what George West would do or say, and the show certainly did not follow the pattern laid down by tradition. What really mattered was that each house was filled to capacity and it was standing room only.

Actually George West held the fort in The Princess's for over 20 years, having first appeared there in 1924. It is interesting to note that in that cast was a double act "Yorke and Morgan". This was the start of Tommy Morgan's rise to fame. He truly deserved his title of the uncrowned king of Christmas, New Year and Easter pantomimes, for even the daffodils had withered before his shows had their nostalgic closing nights.

Without any doubt The Princess's Theatre was a symbol of Glasgow, a part of old Gorbals, and a way of life.

Things were in direct contrast when I worked with Dave Willis in the Theatre Royal pantomime in Glasgow. The show had a traditional title, "Goldilocks and the Three Bears", and followed the story to the letter.

Dave Willis was one of the kindest people you could wish to meet, and working with him was a revelation. His timing was meticulous. He carefully studied his scripts and perfected the gags with a dedication such as I had never seen before.

I was engaged to work with him in his comedy sketches, a change for me, but one I thoroughly enjoyed as I have always had a leaning towards comedy. In many shows I regretted that I had to be the singer when I would much rather have been assisting in raising laughter.

The principal girl was Trudi Binar who came all the way from Austria, and had a fascinating broken accent. She made the ideal Goldilocks with her long golden curls and sweet smiling face. I don't think many people will remember Trudi, for she found our climate too rigorous, but I have always remembered her unusual name and attractive personality.

Also in the cast were comedians Jewel and Warriss. To be truthful, I didn't find them the easiest couple to get along with, but that may have been because they were none too sure of a Scottish welcome, and time did mellow them when they came to understand the Scots and the intimacy which emanates from a Scottish audience.

A husband and wife team, Florence Hunter and Cliff Harley, were also in the cast, and this proved rather an embarrassment. Two Florences and both vocalists! However, I did very little singing in that show, but learned a great deal about the intricacies of comedy, and exactitude of timing.

The Theatre Royal never possessed the homeliness of The Royal Princess's Theatre. I always had the impression it was a purely business venture which lacked the warmth so essential to an artiste, whereas in

The Princess's it was the artistes who were given every consideration and made to feel a cherished part of the organisation. Doubtless The Princess's had spoiled me for other shows.

I had a tremendous respect and regard for wee Dave Willis. He was the comedian who made thousands laugh, and, occasionally, shed a tear. Born in 1895, he died in 1973; was a natural comic, a very hard worker, dedicated and brilliant, for he could switch from comedy to pathos simply by raising an eyebrow. I've seen him come off stage thoroughly exhausted, yet, after a short rest, get up, crack a gag and make for the stage once again to do battle. Believe me he worked like no other comedian I have seen. I often wondered how he must have felt knowing that his first date had been in the self-same Theatre Royal, only on that occasion he was merely a member of the chorus.

I was extremely sad to learn in later years that he'd lost all his hard-earned savings in his Rothesay hotel. Dave was an artist. He had never been forced to exercise administrative ability, hence his downfall. All his working life it had been a case for him of "on with the motley, the paint and the powder" and in that field he will always be remembered with much affection. I will never forget him telling me in a nostalgic moment that the great Chaplin had once told him he was the greatest wee comic in Britain. This I heartily endorsed.

Pantomimes are thrilling experiences. There is the joy of bringing laughter to excited children, there is the happiness in making even a temporary escape route from worry for their parents, and there is always the knowledge that with Christmas approaching, you can play a big part in promoting its real meaning, for Christmas is a time of goodwill, of happiness—and of laughter.

Pantomimes are the stepping stones to the most wonderful season in the year. My hope is that they never cease.

THIS WAS MY RUM

Archie Cameron was born on Rum and describes himself and his two sisters as "the last three genuine Rumonians left". This extract is from a sheaf of reminiscences of life on the island as he knew it at a time when it was owned by the wealthy English industrialist Sir George Bullough.

My father went to Rum as a young man and was employed there in various capacities for 46 years. He married my mother, who was cook in the White House and I was born there in 1903. The White House was used by Sir George Bullough while the castle was being built and was later the factor's house.

One of my father's first jobs was to attend the machinery that heated the water and pumped it to the turtle and alligator tanks. The turtles were not, as has been said, kept for making soup. They were merely curiosities to amuse guests.

Ultimately they proved more expensive than anticipated, for one day, when Sir George was leaning over their tank, the diamond ring he was wearing dropped in. I have no doubt that the diamond was of the same magnificent quality as the other acquisitions from his world tour. The pond was emptied and swept out, but the ring was never found. Perhaps this decided the fate of the turtles for shortly afterwards they were shipped out and released at the back of Canna. Since then there have been several instances of turtles being brought in by fishing nets. Could these be descendants of the Rum turtles? Is there still one swimming around with a diamond ring in his stomach?

The alligators were kept in a deep tank in one of the glasshouses and when the reptiles were disposed of, the tank was roofed and carried pot fruit trees of various types. The alligators did not bite through the iron railings as is sometimes alleged; the creatures were, after all, not more than three feet long.

Partridges were a venture which failed for some unknown reason. Of the first and only brood introduced, one single bird survived for a few years. This was a cock which, finding himself bereft of kith and kin, took up residence with our hens and looked upon them as his own flock. One day, I heard a commotion in the field near the house and rushed out to see the hens and chickens flying off in all directions, squawking and screeching. Not so the gallant little cock. He was battling furiously with a hawk which was attempting to make off with a chicken. I rescued the brave wee bird, but he was so badly injured that he died from his wounds shortly afterwards.

Pheasants were a fairly successful venture. However, they made a bit of a nuisance of themselves and during the run-down of the estate were shot as vermin. The patches of arable land were very small and as their natural free range was very limited, the birds attacked the crops of grain and corn. Blackcock were brought in, too, but, as might have been foreseen, they died from starvation. These birds live mainly on conifers, and at that time these were in very short supply on the island.

When his enthusiasm for strange creatures faded, Sir George became more and more interested in the wild ponies which roamed the hills. He made energetic and prolonged efforts to "improve" the breed, even to the extent of introducing a white pure bred Arab stallion. The "improvement" certainly produced some remarkable colours, such as various shades of cream and gold with chestnut manes and tails and vice versa. The Rum ponies are not therefore a strain unadulterated since the time of the Norsemen's occupation of the Western Isles as is often claimed, but it is to their credit that they have been able to revert to the appearance and characteristics of the breed despite dilution over many generations of their forebears.

At one time the ponies, when walking through the glens, took the easy way and walked on the well-surfaced roads. Now, like the less nimblefooted pedestrians, they must walk on the grass verges as the roads are no more than dry river-beds.

Although Sir George himself disdained transport and preferred to walk several miles before reaching his stalking area, he made every provision for the comfort and convenience of his guests. Apart from the two glistening Albions which would clock up approximately 100 miles a year, there was the harness room, stocked with everything from side-saddles to snaffles. He had the horses, too, to carry these accoutrements, but they were rarely used. Lady Bullough's own horse, Pebbles, a beautiful palomino, was used to pull the "machine", a jaunting car which provided a very pleasant means of travel, with an unrestricted view of the countryside.

The final peak of affluence, in my opinion, however, was the two luxurious four-wheeled, horse-drawn carriages. Perhaps this opinion was created by the fact that these beautiful vehicles with their deep blue upholstery and the Bullough monogram on the door panels were kept in comfortable seclusion. They were used, I think, only once, as it was found that the two horses were unable to pull them up the "Big Brae". Since it was the only road on the island apart from those round the Castle, there was nowhere else for them to go. Mould and moths ultimately finished them off.

While on the subject of transport, I should mention here the experiments carried out in his spare time by Fred Cottrel, one of the chauffeurs. I do not know if these were sponsored by Sir George, but they must have been, at least, approved. Fred tore up and down the loch in a fourteen-foot boat, driven—or rather drawn—by an aerial propeller which looked very dangerous as it whirled round above the heads of the passengers. This long, narrow boat was one of two which Sir George had brought home from wherever he did his tarpon fishing. He also brought home one of the tarpons, about eight feet long and, of course, stuffed. He apparently did not like the look of it in cold blood and presented it to Neil McLean, one of the islanders, and it occupied the whole wall on one side of his sitting room for a long time. A gruesome and greasy-looking object.

The tarpon fishing boats were very fast, but extremely fragile and had to be handled with great care. There was competition to obtain one of them to take us to our fishing grounds, which could be six or seven miles away. We—none of us over 15 years of age—rowed these boats as hard as we could pull, racing the other boat to be there and back home before them. We could row better than we could walk. And we could walk!

The tarpon boats went out of my ken along with Fred and his propeller, but I would love to know if he carried on with his experiments after he left Rum. Perhaps he progressed to hovercraft!

It has been said that the roads were in

Lady Bullough's drawing room at Kinloch Castle gives some idea of the splendour in which the family lived on the island.   PHOTO: CHRISTOPHER K. MYLNE

such good condition that cars could travel to Kilmory, a distance of five miles, in five minutes, but I don't think this is true. It is questionable if the early model Albions, although beautifully maintained, could achieve 40 mph and the "Wee Brae", "Big Brae" and "Devil's Elbow" had to be taken in first gear. Compared with present-day travel, it was a pleasant and peaceful trundle with the weekly laundry to Kilmory. The beach there is one of the best on the west coast. A mile of white sand without a footprint. During the Great War a ship was sunk nearby and the beach was littered with hundreds of cases of sheep and pig carcases. What was left by the gulls was ultimately buried by the drifting sands.

In this area, attempts were made to introduce hares. They were of the southern variety and loped about for a few years. Another attempted introduction that failed was frogs. The head gamekeeper maintained that they were all eaten by ducks before they had time to regenerate themselves. This is possible as mallard ducks were at one time bred there for sport.

In Kilmory is the old cemetery where can be seen a headstone bearing the names of seven children who died within one week. They were the family of the shepherd and the accepted explanation of the tragedy was that they had found a bundle of clothes washed up on the beach. The children wore them and contracted some fatal disease.

Another event I recall does not concern

death, but survivors. The men rescued from a wrecked boat were distributed among the houses at Kinloch. Those who were given shelter in Neil McLean's house were entertained with fiddle music by their host. Many years later, one of Neil's sons emigrated to Australia. One night at a friend's house a stranger asked him if his father played the fiddle. The man was one of the survivors of the wreck.

Wrecks were frequent on the west side of the island which was exposed to the full fury of the Atlantic, but despite the heavy rainfall in Rum it was not incessant, and Rum, like many of the Western Isles, enjoys much better weather than many places on the mainland.

Doubts have been cast on the amount of sunshine required to ripen the fruit in the glasshouses, but I can assure any cynics that it was sufficient to ripen the two houses of Black Hamborough and two houses of Muscatel grapes, two houses of figs and six of peaches and nectarines. It was my duty, as one of the fourteen gardeners, to rake up the fallen ripe peaches on a Saturday morning, shovel them into a barrow and wheel them out to the dump.

Sir George was ever diligent in his efforts to make Rum a place unique in the Western Isles, if not in the whole of Scotland, while at the same time never losing sight of the comfort and convenience of his guests. This included as much entertainment as it was possible to provide under the somewhat restricted circumstances area-wise. He had even laid out a bowling green and golf course in the policies surrounding the castle. The latter was quite a benefit to us youngsters as we periodically crawled through the shrubberies for lost balls. The large fountain in the lawn in front of the castle was also fruitful. We used to plunder it, poaching the trout with which it was stocked, but only after dark for it was in full view of the front windows. The balls we cut up to get at the elastic with which we made catapults.

The castle and its occupants were to us the centre of the universe. Sir George and his lady were the most kindly and courteous people. The story that is told of Lady Bullough offering the butler a damaged sandwich is rubbish. I have nothing but very pleasant memories of that gracious lady. Sir George in his kilt of Rum tweed or Mackenzie tartan was an imposing figure of 6ft. 8in. and well built.

Of course, there is always a fly in the ointment. In this case it was the factors. All their vile actions were attributed to Sir George until their deception was revealed and they were removed from the island.

It was significant of the relationship between us and the proprietors that those close to them remained there all their lives—unless they fell foul of the factors. My father was sacked once for no given reason, but when Sir George heard about it in some roundabout way, it was the factor who went and my father was reinstated. It was a serious business being sacked, as you had to vacate your house and leave the island and if you did not have relations on the mainland who could give you temporary residence, you were in deep trouble. All these sackings, I may say, were done in the laird's absence. Often when he returned and noticed the new face—usually a friend or relation of the factor's—it would be too late to rectify matters.

Eventually the factor's post was given to Duncan McNaughton the head gamekeeper, who carried out his duty faithfully and amicably until his death, when the island was handed over to the Nature Conservancy. One of McNaughton's duties was to rouse the "establishment" with his bagpipes, marching round the castle every morning. We used to set our clocks to the sound of "Johnny Cope" at eight o'clock. His predecessor, and the first piper to perform this duty, was the late Neil Shaw, the founder of the Highland Association. Neil was a steward on Sir George's steam yacht the *Rhouma* and was rowed ashore every morning to pipe round the castle.

The arrival of the *Rhouma* was the highlight of the year. The mechanics and chauffeurs would be there with the two highly-polished Albions. The deer ponies would have been broken in ready for the moors. Fishing lines and creels would be in first class order for the supplying of the daily fresh fish and lobsters. Roads would be freshly resurfaced and the boats delivered to the various hill lochs by horse-drawn sledges. The four gamekeepers and gillies would be dressed in their new issues of Rum Tweed and the whole island would feel alive. Soon we would have enough venison to last us until the gentry returned the following year.

The Rum Highland Games were the highlight and culmination of the season. There were all the events associated with traditional Highland Games, with some of the guests taking part. There were three tug-of-war teams. One from the *Rhouma*, one from the gardeners and the third composed mostly of farm workers, game-keepers and gillies. The last team always won. Old Sandy was their anchor man and when the pull was over, his cry could be heard resounding through the crowd, "That's the fresh herrings, boys!" These fish were plentiful and were Sandy's staple diet, when available.

Many well-known names were among the assembly and the competitors on this day: Lord and Lady Morton, the Cadogans, Sir Donald Currie, and Lily Elsie the beautiful actress wife of Sir George's brother Ian.

Sir George was a handsome figure as he strolled about the field with his cromag. Neil McLean was the announcer and rang the bell to warn the competitors that another event was about to commence. This meant a scrambled rush from the tower where a barrel of beer lay on trestles and it was self-service for all. When the tower was vacated and the erstwhile occupants were running and jumping about the arena, we youngsters would creep out of the shrubberies to empty the glasses, put down in haste. It was delightful stuff compared to what is called beer now.

The tower was an ornamental building with artistic leaded windows. It had been built to house African weapons and relics of the Boer War. Spears and shields adorned the walls among guns of all sizes. Shells of various calibres were also on display on the floor and shelves. The building stood intact until a few years ago when a party of boys from a well-known school visited the island. When they left, all the windows were smashed. So much for education.

One of the more athletic of the guests was Major Poole who did a circuit of the island—approximately 30 miles—and challenged anyone to beat his time. James McAskill, a gamekeeper, took it up and did so, winning a considerable sum of money and a gold watch for his performance. I doubt if he thought the reward was worth the effort though, as he was a sick man for long afterwards.

These house guests had, of course, to be catered for and the sweating kitchen staff who did so were ruled over by mercurial French chefs who were notoriously short-tempered. They were seldom able to speak much English and their attempts to make themselves understood seemed to rouse them to fury. I just escaped being trampled one day by a fleeing kitchen girl, pursued by the chef waving a large carving knife. In the kitchen, everything seemed to be done to constant cries of "Toot sweet!" I did not know then what this meant, but it certainly created a sense of urgency in all who heard it.

The really big day for the juveniles was the picnic to Kilmory. We were taken there in the two luxurious Albions, and we loved the smell of leather and petrol. There was a matter of protocol, and maybe prestige, connected with travelling in cars. One had a high hood and the other was open—the girls' and the boys' cars—and it was considered unmanly to be seen sitting in the hooded car.

What a wonderful sound they made— droom, droom, droom, increasing in rhythm when they got on to a straight bit of road. The carts followed up with the food which included home-grown melons, strawberries, peaches and grapes in abundance. It was a tiring but wonderful day.

Despite the scarcity of feathered game on the island, Sir George was equipped as if to deal with vast numbers. He had a pack of 24 black and tan game dogs. This breed was *the* dog then, but there was little work for them and it was a rare event to see two of them out to walk up the odd grouse. The whole pack was taken for exercise every morning and what a terrifying experience that was for the children as this parade always coincided with school time. I am sure that many big game hunters have been less frightened by a pride of lions than we small children were by this pack of dogs milling around us. There was one dog in particular, Dinah, who would rush up showing a mouthful of glistening fangs. This was really terrifying and with shouts of, "Dinah, Dinah!" and cracking of Donald McGilvary's whip, poor Dinah was driven off. I later realised that poor Dinah was the friendliest dog in the pack, but she had this unfortunate way of showing it.

There was, at times, a smattering of fox hounds and beagles which were taken out on their own. There was no work for them on the island and it would seem that they were brought there for a holiday. The black and tans, beagles and all, gradually dwindled to one liver and white pointer called Broom who spent a very happy life pointing woodcock and snipe for the solitary gamekeeper.

Lady Bullough was not very enthusiastic about Rum and the sporting life that it provided. She was French, very much a socialite and enjoyed a bit of chit-chat and gossip. Her first call, after she arrived on the island, was always to our house where she and my mother gabbled away all afternoon, inquiring about, and no doubt into, the life and affairs of their mutual friends. She knew all my mother's friends and my mother knew most of hers, having been in the service of the Bulloughs for many years.

Although Lady Bullough did not take to the hills as some of her female contemporaries did, she, and they, did not lack from indoor entertainment after the sporting members had discarded the blood and mud of the day's activities.

Dancing in the ballroom under the heavenly blue ceiling with its astral decorations to the sounds of the amazing contraption, the electric organ, was a favourite entertainment and a scene of fairyland to those of us who were permitted a peep at how the rest of the world—and especially our gentry—lived. While these jollifications were going on, the head gardener and I set up the table decorations in the dining room. The high table would be laid out as a miniature garden, with different designs and colours each evening. We were not popular with the tablemaids and I am sure our artistic efforts were not appreciated by them, on account of the slabs of peat into which we stuck our flowers to simulate little flower beds. We were, however, always compensated on the following day by receiving compliments and thanks from her Ladyship.

Apart from the ballroom activities, there was also boudoir music for the ladies. When the gentlemen retired, or escaped to the gun-room, various imported artistes would perform for the ladies. The only member of these individual performers whom I can recall was McNally who was at that time, I believe, the leading dulcimer player in the country. So proficient was he on his instrument that he invariably covered it with a black velvet cloth and struck the keys through this. Perhaps my reason for remembering McNally in particular was that many years later I came on him entertaining a different class of people: Glasgow folk going doon the watter on a Clyde steamer. He was quite an old man then, but had not lost the ability to produce lively dance music on his dulcimer.

The saga of the Bulloughs is ended, but many of the treasures remain and the most interesting and, I believe, the most valuable was "liberated" by the Nature Conservancy when they acquired the island and stored in Edinburgh. This should have a special place in Kinloch Castle where it rightly belongs. I refer to the Ivory Eagle. The creator of this marvellous work of art spent his whole life making two identical figures. One was in the possession of the Czar of Russia and has now disappeared, no doubt destroyed during the Revolution. The Rum specimen is the only one known still to be in existence. I believe that each feather on the life size model was individually carved and placed in position and every detail is perfect.

It would be far more appropriate to have it back where Sir George meant it to be—in his fabulous castle on the beautiful Island of Rum. ▣

SCOATCH BROATH AND AIPPLE TERT

Maureen M. Reynolds remembers her experiences working in a Dundee restaurant which became something of a legend.

It was on a hot May morning in 1954, just two months short of my 16th birthday, when I first became acquainted with Wallace's Auld Dundee Pie Shop. Due to the vagaries of the American sweetie-eating public, a 100 or so employees of Keiller's sweet factory had been laid off when an export order failed to materialise. I was one of them, and with all the confidence of youth, I had decided to bestow my limited talents on Mr Wallace's establishment.

Being young, with a head full of teenage nonsense, and knowing nothing about the long, distinguished history of this city landmark, I must admit my first impression was unfavourable. As I gazed at the drab facade painted in nondescript brown, the warm sun reflected off the large window, but because it was backed inside with a sheet of hardboard, the golden fingers of light failed to displace the dull grey lifeless look. I tried to peer through the front door, but the interior was hidden behind a varnished wooden screen. There was a faded, old-fashioned aura about the place, a mixture of dowdiness and genteel decorum, as if the world had passed it by.

Still, the restaurant's Rip Van Winkle appearance didn't extend to Wallace's bakery shop next door as it was extremely busy. A large straggling queue snaked into the street where prospective customers stood in an untidy line to await their turn. Harassed women, their faces flushed in the unaccustomed heat, scurried out of the shop clutching white paper bags containing hot pies and bridies, the scalding fat making round opaque circles where the paper touched the juicy contents. A succulent smell wafted out and swirled tantalisingly towards the waiting queue, no doubt sharpening their taste buds in anticipation.

Taking a deep breath I pushed open the door and stepped from the glare of the sunlit pavement into the dim, cool silence. Against acres of dark wood-panelled walls, rows of white-clothed tables set with gleaming cutlery and glasses stretched out before me in stiffly starched lines. In the deserted hush it resembled a scene from the *Marie Celeste*. Little did I know then that this was the happy halcyon hour, the calm before the storm, a peaceful hiatus between the frantic morning trade and the frenetic lunchtime crowd.

Sitting in this churchlike gloom, sipping tea from a delicate china cup, and waiting to interview me, was Mr Alf. He was a friendly, dapper man with a kind, modest unassuming manner and I liked him immediately. I didn't meet Mr Ron, who, as well as running the business jointly with his brother, also did the firm's book-keeping which he dealt with in his minute office sandwiched between the shop and the kitchen.

I was a bit dismayed when the wage of 30/– was mentioned as this was 10/– less than my previous job, but I cheered up when Mr Alf said I would have my tips. He went on to explain that the dining room was divided into groups of four or five tables called stations, and every week, the waitresses moved from one station to the next. At the back of the main room were two smaller ones, each containing tables. Mr Alf explained: "We normally reserve these for people who come every day. There are customers who have been eating here since we opened in the Twenties." His face showed genuine pleasure at the thought of such loyalty.

As we were mutually satisfied with each other, a Monday morning start was agreed. I was just about to leave when he pottered off to fetch Miss Thomson, the manageress. I waited apprehensively, still not sure if this was the right move for me. In that fuddy-duddy atmosphere and quiet stillness, I couldn't imagine anyone under 50 working there, though I fervently hoped there was.

When Miss Thomson appeared in the doorway, my heart sank. To say she matched her surroundings was an understatement. Apart from a creamy, crochet-frilled collar clasped at her neck with a cameo brooch, she was dressed entirely in black. It was difficult to say how old she was, but to my young eyes she looked ancient, and although she was small and stooped, there was a sharp birdlike quality about her. She could have stepped straight from the pages of a Jane Austen novel without so much as changing a curl. Behind her spectacles, her black-eyed gaze swept me, noting with disapproval, my sleeveless blouse, cotton dirndl and bare legs thrust into open-toed sandals.

"Be here sharp at eight on Monday,

dressed in black with a white apron, collar and cap." Her voice was soft and sibilant with a slight hissing sound. As an afterthought, she added, "And make sure you wear stockings—we don't allow bare legs in this restaurant."

My heart sank even further when I realised that amongst my handful of outfits there was nothing that remotely resembled black, but I wasn't going to tell her. Over the weekend, Mum managed to rattle up a simple skirt from a discarded garment. As she sewed, she chattered on about my new job.

"Eh remember the peh shoap when it wiz in The Vault—that wid be in the faither's time. Ye ken, it wiz alwiz such a braa treat fir iz when yir grandad brocht hame pehs fir the Setterday denner. Eh kin also mind when, during the war, fowk wid queue richt doon Castle Street and intae Exchange Street, jist tae get their pehs."

In 1892, David Wallace had opened a small baker's shop in the old Vault area of the city centre behind the fine old town house. His simple philosophy was to work long hours, and stay open when his competitors were closed. His penny pies, made with the best chopped meat and seasoning, enclosed in a hand-made pastry case, were not only nutritious, but good value for money.

In spite of these sterling qualities, the business almost collapsed on the first day when his total sale was one pie. In a fit of despondency he walked to the docks and threw the shop key into the murky water. Fortunately, his wife was more optimistic, and she persuaded him to have a new key made and so the Auld Dundee Pie Shop was saved.

Mrs Wallace's optimism wasn't misplaced. Business was brisk as the pies, and later on, bridies, became a main part of working-class family diet. As trade prospered, new branches were opened. By the start of the Great War, the shop and bakery in Broughty Ferry, which included the Loftus tearooms, were thronged with day trippers as they headed for the beach on sunny summer days.

With the demolition of The Vault, the business moved in 1924 to Castle Street and the site reputed to be the former premises of James Chalmers, inventor of the adhesive postage stamp. It was during the General Strike of 1926 that David and his two sons, Alf and Ron, expanded by opening a bakery and restaurant in addition to the shop. With transport at a halt, one of the sons had to go to Edinburgh by car to obtain supplies, but in spite of these difficulties the business prospered. Sadly, within two years of the Castle Street opening, David died, but his sons carried on the family tradition of good value and service and the original pie and bridie recipes were retained.

By the late Thirties there were nine shops dotted around the city, and the Wallace success could be gauged by the fact that the bakers could work up to a 100 hours a week and regularly turned out, on a Saturday alone, 10,000 bridies and 100 dozen pies. Unfortunately, wartime meat restrictions saw the closing of some of the branches and by the early Fifties, all the baking and most of the trade was concentrated in Castle Street.

On Monday morning, sharp at eight, I was back at the shop. The early morning light cast a pearly opalescence over the brown-painted stonework, making it appear even more faded and bypassed. The door was locked, but in answer to my loud chapping, an impish face topped with black curls appeared. She danced around, throwing hand signals like a refugee from "What's My Line?", and after a few gestures, I realised I was meant to enter by the close.

The original pie shop in The Vault. It opened in 1892 and moved to Castle Street in 1924.

This ochre-painted passage led onto an internal courtyard, and as I hurried along, the babble of men's voices and grey wisps of cigarette smoke drifted out through the slats of a corrugated iron shed. It was the bakers having their after-breakfast smoke and enjoying a rest after a busy night in the hot, stuffy bakehouse. At the foot of the bakery steps, Nan, the owner of the curls was waiting for me.

In the dining room, bustling about on the early morning chores, were Margaret and Marion. It was a relief to see they were in their early twenties. Nan handed me a pile of newly-laundered tablecloths, the fresh crisp damask starched to a satiny sheen.

"Mak shair ye always keep yer tables clean, Miss Thomson is awfy fussy" she said cheerfully.

First impressions had proved hopelessly wrong. My working time with the firm was to be one of the happiest and busiest periods of my life.

Miss T. appeared at nine and immediately collared me. I tried hard not to fidget under her stern gaze as she lectured me about the job.

"Young lady, you are now working for a long-established family restaurant, famous for its service and quality. People from all over come here to eat and we pride ourselves on being the best." Her stern words left me in no doubt that I had to toe the line. Any hopes I had about being treated as grown-up were dashed when she asked my age. "In that case," she said, "we'll call you 'The Bairn'."

At lunchtime, she put me on two small tables tucked close to the sideboard, where, with suppressed eagerness, I awaited my first customer. He was a tall, thin, gaunt man, dressed in working overalls and with an impatient frown. After gazing sourly at the menu, he snapped, "Scoatch broth an aipple tert, pleeze."

In the kitchen, I was handed a large plate containing a chrome metal bowl full of soup. As I placed it reverently in front of Mr Gaunt Face feeling decidedly pleased with myself, he gave a peculiar look but said nothing. With his first mouthful, Margaret hurried by and whispered in my ear, "Ye're supposed tae empty the soup oot o the bowl intae the plate. Watch oot fir Miss T!"

As I took a step towards the poor man, I could hear the toe-curling sound of the sharp metal spoon scraping across the bowl. Glancing around the room in a panic, I was sure every screech must be heard by the sharp ears of the manageress, but luck was with me. By now the waiting queue

I placed the soup in front of
Mr Gaunt Face.

stretched into the street, and she was too busy slotting people into vacant chairs like some gigantic jigsaw to pay much attention to me. I hovered around my customer, watching every mouthful and desperately willing him to finish so that I could whisk away the offending bowl. Dressed in my black and white, I must have resembled an agitated penguin escaped from the zoo. When he collected his bill, the customer's gaunt features had a grey ashen look and I don't think I ever saw him again.

Within ten minutes of lunches starting, the place was bulging at the seams and I was kicking myself for ever thinking it was bypassed. It seemed as if the entire population of Dundee and district dined at Wallace's. By 6.15 p.m., my feet were on fire, my legs ached, but my tips total was 1/3d. Not bad for a first day.

As soon as the restaurant opened at nine in the morning, people would arrive in droves, to have a snack and meet their friends. Next morning, with a list of Miss Thomson's do's and don'ts ringing in my head, I watched as my first three customers approached. The two women waddled towards me with a rolling gait, their serviceable brown tweed coats belted tightly around their ample bodies, and pink plump faces flustered and ruffled with the morning sun. Behind them, a timid-looking man, weighed down by a black rexine shopping bag full of groceries, followed wearily. Assorted shapes wrapped in Maypole paper bags peeped out from the unzipped slit. As they eased themselves into their seats, the plumpest woman sighed so loudly it was like steam hissing from a boiler. "Oh, it's braa tae tak the wecht aff yer feet. Meh coarns ir killin me," she gasped and sucked in huge mouthfuls of air while wiping her glistening cheeks with a miniscule hankie. I waited while they sorted out their order.

"Richt noo, Eh'm hivven an ingin bridie. Ina, you want a plen ane and Chic wants a peh and beans." At this point she turned, and in a stage whisper exclaimed, "Wull ye mak shair ye put the beans oan the side o the plate and no on tap o the peh as Chic is awfy fussy."

Chic sat quietly in his seat, looking as if he had never voiced an opinion in his life. As I turned towards the kitchen, her voice called after me.

"Wait a meenit, Miss! Kin Eh cheenge meh oarder tae a plen bridie. Eh've awfy hertburn and the ingins'll mak it worse."

"Goash, are ye aa richt, Bella?" asked Ina, clucking sympathetically in her friend's direction, while Chic gazed blankly at the wall.

If Bella was plump and indecisive, my next two customers were the opposite. Thin as whippets and just as snappy, they made it clear that service was to be instant. Although dressed in similar cotton frocks with a pattern of splendid technicoloured cabbage roses, one woman had the advantage of a newly-permed coiffure. Grey waves and curls set in cement-like rigidity were revealed when she removed her chiffon scarf, while her poor permless friend had to resort to hiding her dinky curlers under a gaudy headsquare printed with ten famous views of Vancouver.

"Twa teas and twa sair heids," snapped Mrs Concrete Curls.

"Eh, a pink ane an a yella ane," barked her pal.

I hadn't a clue what they meant, but luckily, Marion was around. She laughed as she showed me the board of small, round sponge cakes topped with an inch of coloured icing and wrapped in a paper band. "They're called sair heids because the band looks like a bandage."

By now, the kitchen was a hive of activity with lunchtime preparations. Earlier in the day, Dougie would bring all the meat required from his butcher's shop in Exchange Street. The chef was busy manoeuvring huge ashets of steaming steak pies from the oven. Eric, who once told me he was the best fish frier in Dundee, slapped his cod fillets in a creamy yellow batter before tossing them into the smoking blue-hazed fat, where they spluttered and hissed.

Filtering through from the shop came the constant tinny ringing noises of the cash registers, while young bakery apprentices with boards of pies precariously balanced on their heads, zig-zagged between the kitchen activity to deliver extra supplies to meet the voracious demands of an everlasting queue. On their return journey, they left a second trail of floury footprints in their wake, much to the annoyance of the kitchen staff. A clanking muffled sound drifted up from the bakery as the bakers, working like beavers under the watchful eye of master baker Charlie Martin, kneaded and rolled huge amounts of pastry dough.

A dozen assorted aromas intermingled and wafted out through the swing door, to a waiting clientele, fortunate that the words calorie and cholesterol hadn't been invented. At the end of the second day, I was the proud owner of 1/6d in tips. At this rate, I would soon be able to buy that fashionable black skirt priced at 19/11d in G.L.Wilson's window.

Wallace's was unique in the fact that, as well as being a busy restaurant, it was also a popular meeting place for people from all walks of life. Mr Ron was a town councillor and every week, his fellow bailies would

In the kitchen, young bakery apprentices zig-zagged with boards of pies on their heads.

meet for a meal and discuss town business. This assembly earned the restaurant the nickname, "The Pie Shop Parliament".

Another meeting occasion was Market Day, when farmers from all the outlying districts came into town. Afterwards, they all poured into Wallace's. There were two rules—everything was cleared from the tables and bills were to be paid at once. This was no slight on the farmers, but as the entire room was filled with a moving mass of humanity with identical ruddy faces, starched white collars and thick tweeds, it was hard to keep track of them. It's said that Chinamen all look alike, but in my opinion the Forfar farmers took some beating. The air was filled with the price of lambs and the farmyard antics of hogs and heifers. We all laughed when Nan, forever the clown, chirped as she dabbed some Californian Poppy scent behind her ears. "Time tae pit oan meh Coty de Coos fir the Farfar fermers."

From the confines of her cashdesk, overlooking this noisy babble, sat Chris, smiling in sympathy as we all dashed around.

My favourite was Andra. As well as holding a conversation with the ten cronies around him, he would shout across the room to his other pals. "Hullooooo, Wull, fit like's yer tatties? Whit's that? Ye're busy pu'in yer neeps."

His boldly checked suit was extra hairy and appeared to be woven from baler twine. I had to resist the urge to pull the inch-long bits of thread that stuck out from the fabric.

One warm afternoon, as I was manipulating the toaster, Alec, one of the bakery apprentices, shouted in through the open window, his words floating over the crackling and sizzling of frying eggs.

"Eh'll tak ye tae the pictures the nicht. Meet me at half-past six under Samuel's clock. See you then, Cheerio!"

Before I could reply, he was gone. As usual, I took my dilemma to Margaret.

"Eh'm no meetin him at Samuel's clock," I wailed.

To generations of Dundonians, this clock was the place where broken dates abounded and was known affectionately as "Duffer's Corner". Margaret had the solution.

"Whit we'll dae is this. We'll saunter nonchalantly tae the tram stop at Thorter Row and hing aboot tae see if he shows up."

We hung about this corner of the Overgate, looking as nonchalant as a couple of Eskimos in a heatwave, and at quarter to seven, we admitted defeat and boarded the tram. As it swung around the curve at Samuels, Margaret peered up Reform Street before dolefully sighing.

"Weel, aa Eh kin say is, if he's there, Eh cannae see him."

Feeling decidedly miffed, I didn't answer, but it all worked out in the end. The next morning the errant suitor apologised for being late—at least, that was his story.

The last time I spent with this happy band of companions was the week that Alec and I got married. Mr Alf made a little speech, while Miss Thomson dabbed her nose with a hanky scented with Devon Violets.

Afterwards, a voluminous tablecloth was wrapped around me and we all marched noisily through the streets, much to the amusement of early evening pedestrians. Bringing up the rear was Pat, banging a huge soup ladle against a silver-plated tray, and as we passed an open window, the strains of Guy Mitchell singing about his "Truly Fair", wafted down. Pat caught the beat with her ladle and we were soon singing, too. It was difficult to say who was the louder, but I reckon that Pat was

Wallace's Pie Shop and Restaurant in Dundee's Castle Street. It was in the restaurant that Maureen Reynolds worked as a waitress in the 1950's.   STAFF PHOTOGRAPHER

the winner by a few hundred decibels.

I visited Wallace's on a few occasions during the Sixties, but most of the friendly familiar faces had gone. Margaret, Pat, Marion and Nan had all moved to pastures new as our lives travelled down separate roads. Only Chris remained, with her reassuring figure still seated behind her tiny cash desk, and with her beam-

ing smile visible over the glass top.

It was with a feeling of sadness that I read about the death of Mr Alf, and I knew his familiar figure would be missed by hundreds of diners who considered him an old friend.

In 1977, after the death of Mr Highland who was co-director, Mr Ron decided to sell the business and retire. It was a sad sign of the inflationary times when he remarked that because of the high cost of ingredients, the humble pie and bridie had become luxury items. What for years had been the staple diet of generations, was now too expensive to produce, and the Auld Dundee Pie Shop bowed out to Kentucky Fried Chicken.

For 85 years, the Wallace family was an institution, a slice of Dundee's history, and their Castle Street shop was a landmark, as much a part of the city's heritage as the Old Steeple and the Tay Bridge. The name was a byword for thousands of satisfied cus-tomers and many an exile made for the shop on a visit home to sample once more a well-remembered pie.

It is now over 30 years since I stood as a youngster on that sunlit pavement, but the warm affectionate memories I have for the restaurant are as fresh as ever. How well I remember one such exile on a visit home, his face alight with pleasure as he ate.

"Eh've nivver forgotten the taste o thae braa bridies," he sighed.

If there has to be an epitaph for the famous Auld Dundee Pie Shop, it is that remark. ▣

WHAT THEY READ THEN

A CURIOUS FACT IN THE
HISTORY OF THE SMALL POX

Paisley Feb 10, 1803

In a parish in Galloway, about forty years ago, a young man died of the small pox. Nine years after, a sister of his died, and was interred in the very same spot. Among other fragments of his body, which had been dug up, there was a part of the scalp which appeared very fresh, and exhibited the marks of the small pox. Curiosity excited some of the people at the funeral to take it up and examine it, and among the rest the person who told me the story. He was then upwards of twenty years of age, and never had had the small pox. On the tenth or eleventh day after the funeral, he became sick, and an eruption of small pox appeared, which continued the usual time, but were very mild. A brother and sister took them immediately after, and from them they spread over the country. Inquiry was made, and at the time, there was no small pox within thirty or forty miles. Such was the account given me by a man, whose veracity I had no reason to suspect.   R.W.

From *The Scots Magazine*, March 1803.

FICTION

THE STRANGER

Agnes Kordylewska

We always sit on either side of the fire, the stranger and I, and watch the logs sparkle and crackle, the bright showers of gold and red flames flying up the wide chimney. When Jeannie, my wife was here, the brass fender glowed and shone, but it's dull now, and her black cat that had the green, slanting eyes, is gone. I rarely leave my seat in the chimney corner, because the high-backed oak settle keeps off the icy draughts that whistle through the cracks in the old doors, that awful wind that howls down the mountainside and into the glen.

I can't remember how long I've been sitting here dreaming about the past, just watching the bonnie pictures in the flames. My bones are old and stiff, and the blood no longer runs hot. When I think how I used to race up the hill from the farm, the blood lusting and wild in the veins, and Jeannie waiting for me at the top . . .

I don't know how long it is since the stranger arrived here. I can't be sure of anything now. My memory plays tricks on me. He rarely moves from that big chair. Occasionally, when I wake up from a sleep, usually after the porridge has been eaten and the left-over oatcakes put back in the girnel, I notice that he has gone. He never says where he is going, or why, but the whine of the wind, the cold teeth of it gnawing at my bones, tells me that the big wooden door has been opened for a second or two.

It's as if a door in my mind opens, too. It's then I think of Jeannie, my parents, my brothers. We had no girls in the family. There was only my mother who provided a soft gentleness for us in the house. My father was a hard man, toughened by too much labour and the cruel winters of the glen. We knew no tenderness from him.

When the door shuts again, my mind is blurred and it's difficult to separate the truth from my imagination.

The night the stranger came, the snow-drifts rose to five feet or more, so I had to let him stay. The fire seems to be the most important thing in his life, and he feeds it all the time. The pile of logs at the back of the house is dwindling, and I feel very uneasy about this. I will have to wait till the thaw comes, till the forestry men get through with their tractor and the new-fangled Land-Rover. Tam Duncan, their foreman, always cuts the firewood for me.

The stranger never speaks about his walks around the house. I suppose he can't get far because the snow is so deep. When he comes back, he goes straight for the fire and sits down again in the big chair. Once I looked out of the window when he went outside, but I couldn't see him. I thought it was odd that I couldn't see any footprints in the snow, but then, he's a strange man.

I asked him a few questions when he came first, but he didn't answer, and anyway, I've got out of the habit of speaking to people. I've been too long on my

[153]

own. He pays no attention to anything. There was that night of the terrible storm that raged down the glen, when the big oak at the top of the road by the kirkyard, the one that was rotten with age, crashed on to the roof of the old house opposite with a thundering enough to wake the dead. He paid not the slightest attention. Once or twice, callers have been here wanting directions, but I never bother to answer and they go away. The stranger seems to sense them coming and he goes out by the back door till they've gone.

I am trying to remember when they took Jeannie to the kirkyard. The papers and the certificates and the like are all in yon old black oak desk of my grandfather's. It's just idle curiosity, as I've nothing else to think about. The stranger says little. Two or three times I heard him whispering, but I couldn't catch the words and when I asked him what he'd said he just nodded and curled his lips in a thin kind of smile.

I don't like to ask him too much in case I upset him. Once he lost his temper because I sat in the old armchair when he wasn't there. I used to sit in it a lot till he came. He jumped up in such a fury that his coat tail blew the sparks in the fire into an angry shower.

All the same I'm glad he's there—he's company and I'd miss him if he went . . .

I woke up suddenly. I think I've been sleeping a lot lately. Every time I waken, the stranger is always there. Sometimes he's staring into the fire. Other times his eyes are on me. I never know what he's thinking.

The porridge is running low, and the oatcakes are nearly finished. Maybe Tam is getting through the drifts. I thought I heard the sound of an engine earlier on. They will bring plenty of porridge and oatcakes. I certainly hear their voices now, so we'll be all right, the stranger and me . . .

This settle is hard on my bones, but the stranger won't be moved out of that chair. My legs feel as if they are frozen stiff. Oh, my God, the fire's out! Never do I remember the fire being allowed to go out! The grate is black, unfriendly, and why did the stranger not see to it? He should never have let that happen. I want to shout at him, punish him for not feeding the fire, but the words won't come. He's getting blurred now, and I can't see him properly. It must be the lack of the firelight . . .

I hear Tam's voice now, ringing out clear in the crisp, white world outside. The door bursts open, and the icy, deathly cold slinks in with him.

"In heaven's name, man, whit are ye daein sittin on that hard settle when there's a comfortable chair ower there? And, wad ye believe, ye've let the fire oot! You were fine when we left you last Friday. Whit's been happening?"

I try to speak, but the words are slow in coming. "The stranger, the stranger wouldn't let me in the chair."

Tam shakes his head, impatiently. "Whit stranger? There's naebody here; you've been dreamin."

Davie, Tam's son, comes rushing in and throws himself into the chair where the stranger always sits, and as quickly throws himself out of it. He is as pale as death. I hear his father say, "What's the matter wi ye, laddie?"

Davie's voice is almost hysterical. "It felt as if something . . . somebody — was in the chair, pushing me. Cold as ice!"

I can see his father is puzzled, but he says, "Dinna be silly, Davie, you're imaginin things."

He leans over me, and I hear him say quietly to the boy, "I think he's had a stroke. He canna move. Gie me a hand here, Davie."

As they lift me, I say to Tam, "I told you there was a stranger here." He answers me as if I were a laddie, though he looks curiously around the room just the same. "Aye, so ye did, so ye did. Now, we'll have to get you down to the cottage hospital."

They carry me to the Land-Rover and prop me up between them. It is bitterly cold, though the sun is shining making the snow sparkle like diamonds. It's slow going, and the tyres crack and crunch on the crisp snow underneath. As we reach the bend at the kirkyard, the vehicle skids and slithers almost into the wall. Tam mutters an oath. I feel dizzy, as if consciousness is slipping away.

Suddenly, I can see every headstone beyond the low wall of the kirkyard. There are the old grey stones belonging to long ago people of the glen, and the white, polished marble ones with ornaments, or maybe an angel, that belong to the graves of long gone lairds. My own family stone stands plain, four square to the wind. My father would have nothing to do with curlicues nor angels. On it are the names of my mother, father, David and Hamish. The other boys emigrated and I don't know if they are alive or dead. Somehow we lost touch. Jeannie's name is there, too, though it seems a long time since I stood and watched her coffin sliding into the hole. How long is it? A year? A month? What does it matter? It's all in the past. All behind me.

At the cottage hospital they lift me gently from the Land-Rover and carry me in on a stretcher. The nurses make me comfortable in a warm, white bed, and I hear them speaking about getting the doctor urgently if he can get through the drifts. My legs feel like lead and I'm cold in spite of the warm blankets.

The nurses have gone. It's all very quiet. Quiet, that is, except for the breathing. There seems to be somebody behind the screen in the corner. I can hear it all the time, the regular rise and fall of breathing. Once or twice I think I've seen a shadowy figure there, but I couldn't be sure . . .

I must have fallen asleep and I've just wakened up. My body is ice cold and I'm shivering under the crisp sheets. I want to cry out for the nurse, but the sound won't come.

Over at the screen I can see something moving. Yes, there is someone there though I can't hear the breathing now. He's coming out and standing in the moonlight. I'm not at all surprised to see it's my friend, the stranger.

I'm glad to see him. He makes me feel very peaceful. He's coming towards me with his hands stretched out as if he's going to lift me up and carry me away.

Where will he be taking me?

⏹

The Scots Magazine is published monthly and may be obtained at all good newsagents or sent by subscription anywhere in the world.

For details, write to *The Scots Magazine*, Subscribers Dept, 7–25 Bank Street, Dundee DD1 9HU Telephone 0382 23131.

INDEX

Numbers in italics refer to illustrations

The ferry from Easdale to Seil Island makes the last journey of the day against the darkening hills along the Sound of Mull.
PHOTO: JOHN RUNDLE